25th Anniversary Edition

The Garden

A Parable

GESHE MICHAEL ROACH

PUBLISHED BY DIAMOND CUTTER PRESS

Reprinted by arrangement with Image, an imprint of Random House, a division of Penguin Random House LLC

Library of Congress Cataloging-in-Publication Data

Roach, Michael, 1952–
The garden: a parable / Geshe Michael Roach—1st ed.
p. cm.
PS3568.O155 G37 2000
813′.54—dc21 99- 046051

ISBN 978-1-937114-46-6

Printed in the United States of America

August 2024

25th Annirvesary Edition

Book design by Rosa van Grieken

Contents

CHAPTER I

The Sun

We met on the feast day of Thanksgiving. Our mothers were friends; her mother had four daughters, my mother had four sons, and they must have met in the market one day and planned the dinner together.

My brothers and I were working near the house that day. We didn't know much of the plan; we were trying to fix a cart, and covered in mud. The daughters rode in each in her own time—the first, the eldest, dismounting in the yard, found us peering out with our smudged faces from under the axle; she was extraordinarily beautiful, black hair, dark eyes. We continued to work half-heartedly after she entered the house, until the second daughter arrived—she was blond, with a strong build, and just as striking. By this time we were up on our feet, trying to brush some of the road off our clothes.

The third appeared then, as if it were a fairy tale, with russet hair, and a laughing face and eyes. Her glance as she passed us to where my mother stood at the front door was enough to make us forget the cart, and begin washing our hands and faces in the trough. Then on a small wagon came the mother, and sitting next to her the last daughter, slender and quiet, with golden curls, and truly seeming like the sun, as the sunlight struck her face, reaching over the back of the house, as the other sun set in red and gold. Then we were all in the home, warm, with candles and meal, and the fragrance of the sisters.

The next morning there was a small pot left behind from one of the dishes they had brought, perhaps the first of accidents that through the course of an entire life seemed less and less like accidents to me. My mother turned and suggested I return it, and looked at me, and again it seemed that in her eyes she was telling me that I should go, and that there was an important reason to be going. I went.

Her mother too looked at me with the same eyes, as she opened the door, and I held out the pot, but in a way that put me a bit inside the door, enough to engage her in some small conversation, which it seemed was planned anyway. And I asked her if the golden daughter could go walking a few nights hence, and she smiled softly, gazing at my eyes with her kind brown eyes, and said that would be good.

First I led by the ways I knew, and she came along, and I felt proud that she did not deny my arm, and the brush of her hair on my shoulder prevented me from seeing much of the way. Then soon we were on another path, one I did not know, and it was quite dark, one of the early winter evenings in the desert where we lived.

This moment marks the beginning of my schooling, not in things of books and classrooms, where I had already spent much time, but in the things that truly matter in the life of a person, and the things that, when we grow older, we realize are most important—the things of the spirit. It was at this moment that I first saw face-to-face the great enemy of humankind, and she showed me, and showed me too the golden warrior who would defeat this enemy, if death does not come first.

She led me into a garden, of stone walls, closed on the western side by a small stone chapel, but all I really saw that first night was a great tree, rare in the desert, with a great wide trunk, and high boughs drooping down, like a cover, against the night, and against the world outside. I leaned my back against the tree, and she pressed herself to me, and along the length of her leg against my own I felt an intense burst of heat, as though it were sunlight itself, an almost supernatural heat, which I have rarely ever since felt come from a human form.

It came into my mind to tell her something of my studies, some ideas from the books I had been with, and to impress her with my schoolboy learning, and to tell her of my growing fame in the school. I opened my mouth to speak . . .

She gazed up, with luxurious doe brown eyes, eyelids half closed, as if experiencing some pleasure I could not see; and I could not speak. I understood only with those languid eyes that my real lesson lay not in the studies, but in mastering myself and my own pride. This I learned at the age of sixteen, from this young girl of younger years, and as if by reward she rubbed her cheek against my chest, and the luxuriant golden hair poured over me, like a waterfall.

I was moved, in a way new for me, and this was the first moment that I knew lust, who would become from that moment on a great and worthy foe throughout my life. I reached my hands up to touch her small breasts, and again the eyes came up to me, open slightly wider, this time with a slight glint of sternness, and I found I could not move my hands. And from these eyes in that moment I learned a second lesson, and felt my heart enter a second place, a kind of goodness.

And she turned, and took my hand, and bade me leave the garden with her, still not having spoken a single word. With that there welled up within me some kind of disappointment, and a hurt; and the moment these feelings made themselves known to me she stopped, and wheeled around, and looked a third time.

I cannot describe what I saw, but I can give some hints; a golden Angel, standing fully erect, arms slightly raised from Her side, palms out toward me, and the golden hair glowing down, framing Her face like a halo, and the face itself glowing in the light of the moon coming from above the carob tree behind us, and soft silken blouse and skirt flowing slightly in the desert wind, and—again the eyes, asking me what right I had to anger, now, or ever again; with Her, or with any living being at all; and was it not my reason for being in this life, at the beginning of this life, at that moment, and from that moment on, only to learn to defeat the darkness of my own mind, and to give life, never-ending life, to the golden light within it.

With this She began my life, as I will tell it here, and as we parted said only, "Go touch the Sun; She will not harm you."

CHAPTER II

Pain

As the seasons passed, She took me to the Garden many times, continuing the lessons that had begun there. It was always at night, and once we had passed the gate She never spoke a word—all the teaching was done with Her eyes, and Her hands, and hair, and touches. The classes fell into a regular pattern. I would be thinking only of Her warmth and scent, and She would be thinking—what, I never really knew.

For hours we would seem like two young lovers, all the moments spent exploring, or resting back on the grass below the carob tree, listening to the sparkle of the fountain, or the few night birds of the desert, or simply feeling the breezes from the desert cross our bodies. Then a thought would come into my mind, some kind of pride, or some kind of desire, or a touch of dislike or hatred, and immediately there would be the eyes, forever half closed in a pleasure unknown to me, suddenly stern, almost accusing; and I would know that She knew what I was thinking, and there would be no choice but to see myself, my mind, as in a mirror, and see the uselessness and impurity of the thoughts, and to simply, quietly stop. And stopping was a pleasure, not only in the stopping, but because in the next moment there would be some reward, as if She were rewarding a child with some candy, for each time my thoughts changed to purer ones I received a caress, or some kiss, or brush of hair. And so I was trained, in the Garden, like a puppy, to watch my thoughts and mind, and to try to make them clean and pure.

The lessons at night had their own rhythm, and pace, and parallel to them continued my lessons in the school, in the learning of the world. The lessons at night seemed a world apart, as they were; but it most often seemed that the lessons of the day were the real ones, the important ones. I excelled, and felt a strength mixed with pride in the excelling, and these feelings reached a peak one day when I received a letter, marked with the seal of the King and signed by himself, inviting me to travel to the capital and to meet the Court there, and to gain admittance to the Imperial Academy. It was the dream of every student in the countryside, and a rare honor for one of us. Clutching the letter, I rode to Her mother's house, to show the Golden One my prize.

It was a rare lesson, and the best I have ever received, on the subject of pridefulness. I will never forget how She looked, for in fact it was one of the last times I saw Her; she was lying back on a couch, half sitting, half lying, with the luxuriant golden hair spread across the back of it, and dressed in a short simple shift that glowed in some kind of silken color, patterned here and there with red roses, made of some Japanese golden cloth, not seen much in our place in those times. I burst in to show the letter with the royal seal and words; I thrust it in Her direction.

"It is from the King himself! An invitation to meet the Court, and to attend the Academy!" But in those brown eyes again I saw no kind of recognition that She had even heard; She only turned the eyes up toward me again, in a kind of utter innocence, mixed with an almost drugged look of pleasure, so like a deer or other wild animal that Her look could be mistaken for simplemindedness, or perhaps omniscience. And there were again no words, only the mirror, by which I saw my own growing arrogance. I was halted but not stopped, and before the year was out I had left, for the capital and my career.

I can say in moments what took years to pass: I digested the capital and Court and Academy, and they devoured me. I learned much, and knew little, from those who were qualified so well to teach me little. I came home with the much honored degree, and felt empty, and a little lost.

I had lost track of Her as well; my mother had died, and my brothers were gone, and with this any knowledge of where She might be. I felt strongly drawn to the Garden still, and sensed strongly that if I went there, and if I could understand that place, then I would meet Her again there, and not have to look futilely in the outside world. So I found a small place to live, to read and do my writing, and took to visiting the Garden at night, spending long hours there walking, or sitting on the wooden bench below the carob tree, or standing near the gate, watching if She might come.

Then one night as I sat there in prayer, praying only for the one thing, I sensed a person approaching behind me in the dark. My heart leapt, and I felt the deep gratitude of a prayer fulfilled, and I turned and looked up in expectation. But the face looking down at me was that of another, and slowly, with wonder, I realized it to be the face of the greatest master of ancient Tibetan learning; it was the face of Tsong Khapa the Great, here before me, exactly as we see it in copies of the original sculptures crafted more than five centuries ago—no handsome face, and no kindly look; not what we expect, or what we imagine as the kind of face that great learning, and infinite compassion, might sculpt—not some serene handsome visage, but rather a look of sternness, piercing eyes on a smallish face dominated by a great nose, like the beak of a hawk, and wide, long ears—above all, a sense of power, mixed with an overwhelming compassion, a demanding compassion, a compassion of action.

"She is not here," he said simply, "or perhaps—anyway, what you see before you is only myself, but I can be of some aid in your quest, and I must be, for you are a person who has surely wasted his life so far, and must surely waste the rest, unless you truly learn the lessons of this Garden."

"But I have not wasted my life," I objected. "I have been to the Imperial Academy, I hold the degree of the Academy, with honors. I am one in a million in our land; no one has gone so far."

"And I say still, you have wasted your life. What can this paper, this degree of the Imperial Academy, bring you?"

"I could become a master of the law, or of medicine, or of any other great and respected profession, and thus win my fortune."

"What fortune?" he asked, and pulled me to my feet before him, and stood before me pugnaciously. And I was a little surprised to see how short he was, and felt somewhat more assured of myself.

"By fortune," I said, "I do not mean great riches; I know of course that this is not the only goal of a life, for this I have studied in my courses in philosophy. By fortune I mean only that moderate amount of wealth that would make a man and his family comfortable."

"And this would not be a waste of life, to have a family, comfortably housed, comfortably fed, in a decent and moderate way?"

"No, of course not, this would be no waste of life, this would be a good life, a full and meaningful life."

With the word "meaningful" he started, and blanched slightly, even in the dark, and fixed his hawklike eyes upon mine, all the more hawklike from the great nose, and then a hawklike grip on my arm.

"So it is not a waste of life, to spend that life only in pain and suffering, and to do absolutely nothing to escape that pain and suffering?"

I was confused. "Of course it would be a waste if it were only pain and suffering, but life is not only that; life has beauty, life has its comforts; a good home, a good family, and the care of one's loved ones and community of good friends."

"So it is not pain," he said, pulling me alongside him, and beginning to walk across the grass to the north wall, near the gate, "it is not pain to break a bone, or to cut one's hand, or to lose one's mother?"

At this I started myself, remembering that same pain. "Of course this is pain, all those are pain, but these pains are not all that life is made of; these pains come now and again, these pains happen on certain days, in certain years, and certainly there is hardly any life, of any person, that is filled only with these pains, and not some beauty and happiness."

"What happiness?" he asked.

"What happiness!" I felt surprised again, for Tsong Khapa the Great in the flesh, this short intense man walking at my side, did not seem the great philosopher at all, and I began to feel some disappointment, not only in his physical appearance, but in his questions as well. "Happiness, well, what about the happiness of a child, a joyful, smiling child?"

"So this is your idea of happiness, the face of a joyful child?"

"Yes," I replied, "of course, this very face. Who could deny its beauty? Who could say this is pain, or suffering?"

He stopped short, and wheeled around at me, and looked up, in a face that held, it seemed, both anger and pity. "This child," he said, "this child. Will it not see terrible things? Will it not see, if it lives long enough, the death of its parents, its dearest father and mother? And will it not see war, and will it not see the hatred and violence done by men toward each other, and will it not see the loss of all that it loves, if it lives so long, and will it not in fact eventually, inevitably, become a toothless, helpless, dying face of an old man?"

I was taken aback. "Of course, of course all these things are possible . . ."

"Possible!" he almost screeched at me. "Possible? Are they not, in fact, quite probable; can we say certain!"

"Yes, I suppose so, very probable, that any child now, however happy, will see all these things, and become himself old, and helpless, a suffering old man."

"So how can you say that the face of the child is beautiful?" he demanded insistently.

"It's obvious," I objected, my objection welling up with complete certainty, naturally, from deep within me. "The child *is* joyful, and the child *is* something beautiful, at that moment, when he looks to us this way. And whether later this child becomes old, and sees the terror and fury of life, still he has, at this moment, in his youth, been joyful and beautiful."

"And so it's a pleasure," he returned, more gently and thoughtfully, "it's a pleasure, and no pain, to slide one's tongue slowly, deeply, across the blade of a razor?"

The image again took me aback, the thought of sliding one's tongue across a razor's blade. "No, of course, it would hurt, it would cut deep."

"But suppose," he said, "the razor were covered with honey; suppose there were a razor hidden beneath a glob of honey, and you licked the honey, and had the pleasure of tasting the warm sweetness of the honey, and did not know the razor was there, and only later realized that in licking the honey, you had slashed your tongue?"

"It would still be a pain, and no pleasure. I can hardly imagine a sharper pain. If in licking the honey, I licked the edge of the razor and gashed my tongue, it would only be a pain."

"So you are saying," he said now with a voice of authority, a voice that made me feel as I did in the Academy, playing chess with a fellow student, and hearing in his voice that I was close to being checkmated, "you are saying that licking honey is not a pleasure."

"Honey itself?" I responded quickly, automatically. "A pleasure."

"But licking honey, when below the honey is a razor which slices your tongue to ribbons—is this a pleasure?"

"No, we have already said that—this is no pleasure."

"So when a pleasure is necessarily and always accompanied by an infinitely greater suffering, then we can say that this is no pleasure?"

"Yes," I said triumphantly.

"Yes!" he said triumphantly, and he showed me the face of the child: joyful, beautiful, and nothing but suffering.

CHAPTER III

Meditation

The words of the master, Tsong Khapa, and I think now the death of my mother, affected me greatly. It was not that I was despondent, or thrown into despair; outwardly I was living a normal life, I continued with studies and writing, making a modest but comfortable living. The walk and the death, though, became constant companions in my mind; each one gave reason for the other.

It was true that my mother had lived a good and fruitful life; raised her children, contributed to her world, provided always and without hesitation for the needs even of strangers that we brought home. But what was the meaning, if regardless of how she lived she grew old, and died so horribly of cancer, and if all that she lived for—her sons, her home, her work—was already crumbling into dust, all to be forgotten, so soon after she herself was forgotten? She was proof of the truth of the words spoken to me by Tsong Khapa in the Garden, that even things which seemed beautiful and good were not so, if death and pain were how they always ended. And in my mind Tsong Khapa existed because of her: he had come to the Garden knowing my needs, and bringing some answers to my questions.

The death and the walk worked on my thoughts over the months, and so finally I was compelled to seek out a small hermitage some distance from our desert town. There I found a kindly, holy, and learned abbot, who gladly took me in, gave me a small, quiet room in which to stay, and secured me work as the assistant to the keeper of a rich collection of books in the manor of a nearby nobleman. I spent much time in the study of sacred texts, and in the thoughts that grew from the walk and the death, and came to feel that there was some path I could learn to solve my questions. I yearned for this path deeply. And so I was drawn back to the Garden, and entered just after dusk one year as the desert was entering its subtle springtime, a slight sweetening of the air, and greening of the spare but lovely grass and rosebushes, within the stone walls of that beloved place. I waited for Her there again.

This time it was no long wait, but as disappointing as it was quick, for I sensed approaching, in the darkness from the gate, a wholly different step from Hers; this one was measured rather than skipping, sprightly but almost businesslike, and above all heavy. I turned and saw the Great Meditator—Kamala Shila.

He was nothing like I would have expected, for I had in mind a severe and austere presence, a face and body that had seen the rigors of deep meditation, hour after hour, on the side of a stone Himalayan cliff, eleven centuries earlier. But here was the real thing, and nothing of the sort. He was of medium height, and chubby, with his robes hitched up too high, nearly to his knees, giving him a sort of playful appearance—like a young boy. His face matched the rest: round, happy cheeks, a full nose, dark Indian complexion, little patches of ill-shaven white hair around the top of his head, and above all laughing, sparkling little eyes, in a constant state of giggling, as was he.

"Want to know the Path!" said he.

"Yes, of course," I replied, for it is a very serious thing to know the true suffering of the world, and to await anxiously for the way of escape.

"Why not!" he laughed, "and—why *not!"*

"I want to know why my mother died," I replied somberly, "and I want to know if there was anything I could have done, or if there is anything still I can do for her—and I want to know if it must always be this way."

"Yes! Yes!" he boomed back. "Can do! *Why not?* Got to learn to meditate!" and he plopped down on that patch of grass beside the carob tree, blessed to me because of the tender nights passed there with Her.

He motioned for me to sit beside him; I had done a little meditation with friends at the Academy, and had read some about it, and so I sat up straight, closed my eyes and tried not to think about anything.

He giggled and slapped me on the back. *"What are you doing?"* he demanded merrily.

"Meditating!" I said.

"Would you run a footrace without warming up first?" he asked happily.

"Well, no."

"Got to do the *warm-up!*" he laughed, and jumped up again.

"What's the *warm-up?*" I said, getting to my feet grumpily, with thoughts of leg stretches and other unpleasant exercise.

For the first time, Kamala Shila looked at me a little sternly. "Everybody wants to meditate! Nobody knows how! *Got to do the warm-up right!*" he said.

"So what's the warm-up?"

"First *clean up!*" he yelled, and began running around the little patch of grass, stooping over his little belly, picking up stray leaves and twigs, until the surface of the grass was smooth and clean in the moonlight, inviting to the eyes, a pleasant place to meditate. "Do this in your room, right?"

"Right," I replied, and started to sit down.

"Don't forget the *gifts!*" he squealed.

"What gifts?" I said.

"Important people coming!" he giggled. "Need some nice gifts for when they get here!"

I glanced dubiously at the gate of the Garden, apprehensive at the thought of a crowd of merry meditators like himself. "Who's coming?" I asked.

"Nobody *you* could see!" he replied, and went over to the wooden bench, and from under the top vest of his robes pulled a bag of tiny little clay cups, which he began arranging in a row. Three he filled with a little water from the fountain, and then went and plucked a small red bloom from atop a thornbush (after what seemed a short prayer, as though he were asking the bush for permission) and placed it in the fourth cup.

From a sage bush and juniper lining the spring that led from the fountain he took a few sprigs, placed them in a fifth cup, and collected a bit of dry grass into the sixth. From the tangerine tree on the near side of the gate he took a fruit, peeled it, placed a few pieces in the seventh cup, and with relish ate the rest, talking as he moved and chewed, pushing a little slice into my hand as well.

"Suppose," he said between bites, "that some very important person were to show up in this Garden tonight, during our meditation. Maybe even a great Queen, with golden hair and a golden crown . . ." And he winked at me slyly, as if he knew why my heart kept me coming to this place. "You'd want to greet them properly, as you desert folk always do for your guests."

"But who are you expecting, really?" I asked.

"*Must* invite the Enlightened Ones!" he giggled. "How can you meditate, if they are not with you? How can you meditate too, unless you bring here, if only in your mind, your Heart Teacher?"

These last words, Heart Teacher, struck me deeply, with some pang in my breast, because the only thing I could imagine when I imagined "Heart Teacher" was my golden Lady.

"Here," he continued, leaning heavily over the little cups, "put them in order, like this. One cup of the water, it's a crystal cup of some wonderful beverage, nice to greet a guest that way."

"Next is another cup of water." He shuffled the little cups around, as if playing a shell game. "That's a warm little bowl of water from one of those mineral springs, nice to wash the guest's feet, tired from their journey."

"Third is the flower. *Everybody* likes flowers!" He took a deep sniff of the fragrance of the bloom. "Next is incense!" and he lit the fragrant leaves in the next cup with a spark from a flint, pulled from the bottomless folds of his vestments.

"Do you always carry these things around?" I asked dryly.

He turned slowly and looked in my face, dead serious. "Want the Path? Got to meditate. Want to meditate? Got to *warm—up!* Of course, I carry them everywhere, and I meditate . . . everywhere!"

He lit the dry grass in the next cup from the glowing fragrant embers. "Nice to light a lamp when a visitor comes. Here now, move that little cup of water next in the row; that's a fragrant ointment that you spread upon the guest—use your imagination now, enjoy it, I'm sure there's some guest you can imagine to whom you would like to offer this scented cream," and he glanced at me from the side, in a strange way, reminding me of someone.

"Now, last in the row, put here the slice of fruit, nice to feed an honored guest." I was wondering when, or even if, we would ever get to the meditation; he sensed, or knew, my thought, and said with a twinge of exasperation, "Must take the time. Must put these gifts out right."

"What, do they actually use them?" I asked curtly.

"Of course not," he said. "You think they, you think Enlightened Ones, need food to eat, or water to drink?"

"Well, if not," I responded, "why put these things out? I thought we were going to meditate."

"Want to run? Got to *warm up!* Can't meditate without them here, can't meditate without your Heart Teacher here, with you, helping, blessing, giving strength. Putting out gifts, it proves—you want them here, please . . . come here, be with me awhile, as I meditate." And then, all of a sudden, Kamala Shila broke into a sweet little song, a prayer song, his face cherubic, uplifted, eyes closed but seeing, as if there were someone there, in the star-filled sky above us, to whom he was making an offering.

He stopped and lowered his face, and looked at me merrily. "That's the last gift, my favorite one to give—always give them some little music, before you sit to meditate."

"And so we can finally sit?" I asked, but tenderly, for no one could deny the beauty, and the feeling, of the place of meditation that Kamala Shila had just created; surely, the Garden, and my own heart, had indeed been *warmed up,* and it felt good, and right, to begin our meditation this way.

"Yes, *why not?* Time to sit!" he exclaimed. I stooped and began to sit, and felt his arm pulling me back up.

"What now!"

"You forgot to bow!" he said, as if surprised that I didn't know better. He put his palms flat against each other at his breast, and bowed with great grace and respect, as if some great being stood before him, and then slowly took his seat upon the grass.

I followed suit and then settled myself upon the grass, but like a little rubber ball he bounced back up again. I was really getting irritated, wondering how late it was getting, and sat grumpily staring ahead. He was flitting all around me, like a bee on a flower.

"Where's your seat? No meditation seat? Must get the back up higher than the front!" and he grabbed my shoulder, pushed me forward, and shoved a wad of cloth (which had appeared mysteriously from beneath his vest) under my tailbone.

Next his hand was on the ankle of my left foot; "Get that up on your right thigh! Sit up straight!" slapping my back straight, "Get that right shoulder down even with the other!" pushing them down level, "Fix the head! Didn't they teach you anything?" I felt ready to strangle the great jolly master.

"Don't point it down, don't point it up, just straight ahead, and stop leaning it to the left!" His two hands were on the temples of my head, like a vise. "How's the tongue?"

"In my mouth, as usual," I retorted. He didn't seem to hear.

"Touch it there slightly, behind the front teeth, keep the mouth loose, everything just natural, like usual," he enthused. "Can't meditate if we're slobbering or swallowing all night, can we? *Stop breathing through your mouth!* You'll dry out!" And he had me completely straightened out, and I had to admit it felt quite good.

"Shouldn't I cross both my legs up on my thighs, like they do in the pictures?" I asked.

"A full lotus? Sure, if you can, but you can't, till you practice more. The main thing is to be completely comfortable, so you can concentrate the mind, without worrying how much your knees hurt. If you want, you can even sit on the bench over there," he explained, and slid down next to me immediately in full lotus.

I closed my eyes, and went into a state of peace, here in the peaceful Garden, the Garden of my Golden One—and he was in my face once more.

"What, you going to bed?" he demanded.

I opened my eyes, and fixed them straight ahead, on a design carved into the side of the wall opposite us.

"You people around here meditate with your mind, or with your eyes?" he demanded again.

I looked at him angrily. "Well, if I'm not supposed to close my eyes, or open them either, then what do you want?"

"Watch," he said, and he sat with his head erect and straight, but the eyes half open, gazing slightly downward, and without focusing on anything in particular, as if he were in some deep reverie, which I realized was the whole point. "If it gets too distracting, you can close them, but your mind is too used to going to sleep when you do, so it might be hard. Make sure though not to open them too wide, or you will start to look around; and see to it as well that the background in front of you is plain, like a cloth or wall of a single color, with nothing moving to catch your eye and distract the mind."

I did as he said, and felt my mind immediately go into a clear state of focus. I prepared to empty my mind . . .

He was up again, running to and fro, and I despaired of ever actually meditating with this, the greatest master of meditation. "What now?"

"Do you hear something?" he asked anxiously.

I let my eyes back down, and concentrated. All I could hear was the familiar tinkle of the fountain.

"Just the fountain, over there against the wall," I replied.

"Got to *go!*" he exclaimed, and headed over to the bench, and made to collect the little cups together.

"What?" I jumped up. "All this work, and now you must go? Can't you stay for just a few minutes, and let me meditate near you?"

"Impossible," he announced. "Noisy, noisy. No good for meditation. Should have noticed it before. Impossible to meditate with noise around," and he pointed to the offending fountain.

"It's not so loud," I said. "Come, try."

Kamala Shila looked at me gravely. "You asked me to show you the Path. I told you there is no Path without meditation. You have to make choices. Your pretty fountain, or your meditation. Your life as it is—and as your mother's life was—or Freedom.

Freedom or your fountain. Your life now will always be such choices. I'm going."

Desperately I looked around, and my eyes caught on the bricks stacked in a circle around the trunk of the carob. I caught one up and placed it on the opening of the fountain, and the water stopped. "Please now, can we meditate together?" I asked quietly.

"Why not!" he giggled, and we sat together on the grass, at peace, and ready to find peace.

The jolly little man transformed then before my eyes. The left hand went down upon his lap, palm up, and then the right one upon the left one, also palm up. The two thumbs touched slightly, a little off the palms. His sparkling face changed instantly, into the very visage of serenity, totally relaxed, totally quiet, a quiet that was so strong that it seemed to suck the entire Garden into it, a realm of total silence. It was a quiet that I hungered for, a quiet that my life had never allowed me, and I sat down eagerly beside him.

For the first time, thankfully, Kamala Shila was quiet, for a few moments at least. And then he whispered, "Did we talk about the *warm-up* yet?"

"Yes, yes," I whispered back urgently, hoping he would settle down. "Remember, we did all that already."

"Not *that* warm-up," he whispered back; "the *other* warm-up."

"What are you talking about?" I said apprehensively, waiting for him to bound back to his feet. But he stayed serene, and led me with his words.

"If you will come with me, into real meditation, you must prepare your thoughts. Otherwise you will be left behind."

"Teach me, please."

"Now first watch your breath, the breathing in and out. See if you can count ten breaths without your mind wandering away. Start with the out-breath, and then the in-breath: this is one breath. See if you can count ten of these; at first, if you are honest, you will not be able to get to ten before your mind wanders off to something else."

I tried, and saw he was right. I never got past four before my thoughts went off, to the Garden itself, and to Her.

"It's enough," he whispered after some minutes. "The point of watching the breath is only to bring your mind to neutral, to pull it slowly away from the whirl of your worldly thoughts, and begin to focus it within. It's not as if watching the breath is itself a goal which would free us."

"Now think for a moment why you are here: you seek the Path, you seek I know to find the answers about the death of a good woman, and about the wisdom you have found from another. Decide now, here, that these questions cannot be answered elsewhere, and in fact are not even asked elsewhere. Children ask why good people must suffer and die, and adults teach their children not to ask anymore, and these children become the adults who tell their children, 'These questions have no answers.' Decide here why you will meditate with me. Decide here, and now, that you will meditate for a real goal, for an ultimate goal, and that you seek these answers in the Path. Do not waste your life, do not waste even the few moments we will spend here together, on any lesser goal."

I reflected on his words, and felt their truth, and felt a joy and rightness in meditating for this one reason.

"Next, before we start to meditate, ask the Enlightened Ones to come; ask your Heart Teacher to come, bring them here, to guide and help us. You cannot see them now, but you will; if they exist at all, if they are who they are supposed to be, they will hear your mind, and they *will* come. Ask them, sincerely, with deep reverence, now, to come, and they *will* come."

I did as he said, and thought I felt Her presence, close to me. My heart leapt with joy and devotion.

"We have bowed to them before we sat; bow again to them now, in your mind's eye, for I tell you, on the day that you *do* see them yourself, you will in one natural motion throw yourself upon the floor, at their feet, in happiness and awe."

Again I did as he said, and it felt good and right.

"Good, good, continue as I say. Sincere people around the world seek to meditate, but find they are unable to reach the depths and heights of meditation, because they have not found how to enter the door of the meditation, which I teach you now. Imagine next then the entire sky."

I did, in my mind imagined the entire expanse of the azure sky of my desert home.

"And fill it entirely with sweet crimson and ivory roses, and offer it to your Heart Teacher, and the Enlightened Ones, and ask them sweetly for their help."

I did, and again, it felt good and right, and my mind felt even closer to deep meditation, even before we meditated.

"Still we have a few steps to go. Clean now your conscience, for no person can meditate unless their conscience is clear. This again is why so many find it difficult to meditate, why so few never see the miracles of the depths of meditation. Your heart must be clean, your life must be clean. Think now of anything you have done, or anything you have said, or anything you have even thought that might have harmed another; admit it to yourself, be totally honest with yourself, decide that you did it, decide that it was not a goodness, and decide that you will try not to do it again. This one cleaning, of your conscience and your heart, will open to your mind doors of meditation that you never dreamed were possible."

I sat quietly, and reflected, not finding any great evils, but many small and daily harms to others, and cleaned them from my heart.

"Good, good. This is *real fun!*" he whispered happily. "Few more steps; now do the opposite, think of all the good things you do, all the good things you've said to others, all the good and pure thoughts you've had and have—oh, and by the way, think of all the goodness of anyone else at all, from your Heart Teacher on down, and just . . . *be glad, be happy, take joy,* in everything that is good."

I did, and it felt a good and proper balance to cleaning my conscience. My mind felt fairly bursting with good energy, and thirsting for meditation, like a warmed horse, about to race.

"Now ask them for guidance—your Heart Teacher and the Enlightened Ones. And ask that they continue to appear to you, in all the many ways that an Enlightened Being can appear (and you can hardly guess all the ways, and all the places, that they appear to you). Ask them to come to you as your teachers, both teachers who seem like teachers, and in the world and the people around you, teaching you, always teaching you, and guiding you along the Path."

With a deep sense of reverence, which drew me already into meditation, I followed.

"And now finally beseech them, from your heart, always to stay near you, seen or unseen, keeping you, and bringing you to them."

This I did, and from the goodness of these thoughts fell into a deep state of meditation, a total quiet. Which, of course, the great Kamala Shila could never seem to tolerate.

"Isn't the peace so nice?" he whispered.

"Oh . . . yes . . ." I could hardly make words.

"And what are you meditating upon?" he whispered back.

"I have emptied my mind, and I am trying not to think, and the thoughts I do have I am simply watching, as they pass by."

Somehow his heavy little body traveled the space between us in a flash, and he was in my face again, this time really angry. "Fools! The fools still live! Fools that I thought I finished off in the great debates, over a thousand years ago! I'm leaving!" and again he headed toward the bench and his little holy cups.

"Wait!" I started up. "What have I done wrong? Teach me what I have done wrong."

He sat down before me, legs crossed on the grass, breathing heavy and intense, and leaning close, his face before my own. Then his look softened, and he asked gently, "Do you want to help your mother?"

"Of course," I said. "You know my quest."

"Then think—what possible good would it be, simply to sit and empty your mind for an hour? Do not animals, like the rabbit, do the same? Are not the drunkards, who pass out after tankards of their mead, just the same? Are their minds not emptied and quieted, for a time? Come, think about it, tell me, why do you think we meditate?"

"Because we seek the truth; and the truth is in the silence of meditation."

"Only half true. Meditation is but a tool, not a goal itself. It is an axe, a sharp axe, with which we cut a tree. Cutting the tree is wisdom, ultimate wisdom, and this is the heart of the Path. Meditating for the sake of meditation would be like burning an axe for firewood, rather than using it to cut firewood. What is the goal of the Path?"

"I hope to find some answer to the question, Why did my good mother die so painfully, why did she die at all, why must we all—good or bad—suffer and die; why does all life, and all the work of life and all the fruits of the work of life, turn to destruction and pain? This is the goal of the Path, for me."

"Good, and so it should be. So now, if you could sit for hours or days or months and empty your mind, would you find the answers—would you be freed from sickness, and the loss of the things and people you hold dear; would you be freed from aging itself, would the energy of your body and mind stop leaking away from day to day—would you not, in a word, die?"

"I suppose I would; I suppose that, even if I could sit here and empty my mind, and be quiet and peaceful and serene even for very long periods of time, and sit even through hot and cold, and rain or the heat of the sun, I suppose you are right, nonetheless one day I would fall sick, and eventually get older and become unable to sit here, and then die."

"So then please," he whispered to me urgently, *"please . . .* follow me now, and learn true meditation, and learn to use it for our real goals." He settled back near me, and this time settled with a finality that I sensed meant he would not rise again.

"There are three ways of meditation," he began, not moving from his own meditation posture. "For the first, I ask you to put before your mind a picture of your Heart Teacher."

This I did easily, and waited easily, for seeing Her, if only in my mind's eye, had always been for me a comfort and consolation.

"The first enemy of meditation," he whispered again, "is a kind of laziness; it is simply not to feel like meditating. And so it is good as we have done to remember the urgent and sacred necessity of our meditation. It is good as well," he giggled, "to choose an object of meditation which is both important, and which we enjoy. I don't think you will have laziness tonight.

"Now I will snap my fingers," he continued, "from time to time. I want you to mark your mind carefully, and tell me where your mind is at the very moment I snap my fingers. This way I can show you the other enemies of meditation, and how to battle with them."

I returned in my mind to my sweet image, and it brought me to thoughts of this Garden, which brought me to thoughts of the hour, which must be late, and I wonder if I will be in any condition in the morning to do my work at the library . . . *snap.*

"Where was your mind?" Kamala Shila asked.

"I lost the picture, I began thinking about my work," I said sheepishly.

"This is the second enemy," he said, "losing the picture. You fix this by becoming so familiar with the picture, by keeping it in mind so often, and on a steady basis from meditation to meditation, in meditations done steadily, during brief but frequent sessions through the day, that you always remember the object, that it is always close to mind. Now go back to the picture."

I did, and was able to hold Her lovely form somewhat better. My body was still, and the Garden still. The meditation felt good. I was beginning to feel comfortable, and more confident. My breath was slow, my body still, and She was always there, a kind of fuzzy golden light . . . *snap.*

"How is the picture?" he whispered.

"Good, good," I replied. "I am still, my body is comfortable."

"No, no," he said sternly, "the *picture*."

"Oh," I said, "it was fine, steady, a little fuzzy . . ."

"Typical," he said, a bit harshly. "Your meditation had slipped into dullness, a great enemy because he is an almost invisible enemy. In the extreme form he is more obvious: you feel drowsy, the head starts to nod. In his subtle form he is pure poison; he lies to you, and tells you your meditation is good, when really you are only in a kind of stupor—many meditators have wasted away a good part of their lives this way."

"So what shall I do?" I asked.

"Reserve a little corner of your mind; we call it watchfulness. Set it aside. Teach him what this enemy looks like; let him know the signs of his coming, and above all instruct him to raise the alarm, to alert you when mental dullness has come to drug your meditation. Now go back to Her."

I was a bit startled to realize he knew the object of my meditation, but settled quickly back. I held Her picture in my mind, and began to reflect on Her beauty, and the many spiritual lessons She had taught me here in this place. I remembered especially the night She had so innocently walked to the water leading away from the fountain, and stepped in without hesitation, clothed in Her golden hair, not crude or unclean, but with a total lack of desire and malice both; simply at oneness with . . . *snap.*

"Where was your mind?" Kamala Shila demanded.

"In good thoughts, holy thoughts," I replied tentatively.

"Good thoughts perhaps, but bad if they disturb your meditation. You wandered from the picture, to some other thought, and some other time or place, something that you like to think about, correct?"

I admitted it was so.

"This is the enemy of mental agitation; this is the one who comes most often, and he is mighty. I need not tell you more. Use your watchfulness, detect his arrival. And I warn you now of his companion, and the companion of dullness. This is inaction: failing to raise your sword when either of these enemies has crossed the threshold of your meditation.

"For dullness, inspire yourself back to fixation upon the picture, and clarity, working first on the outline of the picture, and then the details of the face, the hand, and so on. If dullness continues, put your mind upon a deep blue sky, a very bright and blue sky, let your mind become this sun-washed sky—it will refresh you—and then return. In an extreme case rise, splash your face with cold water, or lie and take some rest, if you must.

"For agitation, gather your thoughts back to your heart, gently, softly. Seek a deeper silence, stay still in mind and body. Slow your breath, count your breaths again if you must, and bring yourself back. Meditation is like the flight of great birds through the sky; as they hover through the wind at a distance, it seems to those of us standing upon the ground that they glide effortlessly. But in fact they are in a state of constant correction, tilting one way as the wind changes, tilting another as the wind changes again.

"Your meditation is similar, and you must continually watch and adjust, keeping it tuned like the string of a lute: not too tight, not too loose. Then finally there comes a time when, with much practice, the meditation is flowing smoothly. This is a time when you must watch for the final enemy, which is adjusting when no adjustment is necessary. Now follow what I have said, and watch the picture again."

I did, and brought Her image back, the true image. I held it clearly and silently, if only for a few minutes, and heard Kamala Shila say, "It is good. Now the second type of meditation, which we call problem-solving. I will give you a problem, and you focus your mind single-pointedly on this problem, and try to solve it. This is an important kind of meditation, and one which will serve you well later."

"I will do as you say."

"Focus now on some small event in your life, something perhaps accidental, but which changed your life, for the better."

I tried, and immediately thought of the pot, the pot that had been left behind at my mother's house on the feast day of Thanksgiving, the pot that had led me to Her door.

"Now consider, whether it was really an accident or not; do we know it was an accident; can we be sure it was an accident; could it have been arranged by someone; what would make someone arrange it; what are the possible motives, common or sacred. Think, consider, analyze, and conclude if you can."

I thought deeply. Considering its eventual effect upon my life, the accident of the pot was certainly very important to me. I had always assumed it was an accident. Even if it were not an accident, it would seem more likely that someone had simply wanted me to meet the girl, and less likely that someone could have known that this meeting would become the door to my entering the path of the spirit; and yet, if Enlightened Ones did exist, and if they truly did see the future, as clearly as we see now the present, then I suppose . . .

Kamala Shila interrupted me here. "It is late; you can consider that matter further on your own, and you must. Learn now the third type of meditation. I want you to review, one by one, the steps I have taught you tonight, beginning from the moment I began to clean the grass of leaves. Go mentally through the whole warm-up, of preparing the place and your own heart, for meditation; and then go through the kinds of meditation, and review the enemies I warned you of, and the ways of defeating them.

"Think lastly of the proper way to end a meditation: imagine a stone, thrown in the center of a pond, and see the ripples, going slowly out. The night we have spent together here, and each one of your meditations, is the same. It is an event, a sacred event, that has repercussions beyond what you can imagine; try to be aware of these ripples, think of them, and pray that they swiftly become waves of help and happiness that touch every living thing around you."

And I began the review, as he had instructed. He sat silently next to me, deep in some meditation of his own. And afterward the final question came to my mind, "But what is it, Master Kamala Shila, that I should meditate upon? What picture or problem or review in my mind can answer the questions we have spoken of?"

"Begin where we must always begin," he answered. "Picture your Heart Teacher before you, and let the picture become perfect to the point of real. Ask Her then for Her help, have faith, and perhaps," he said, with a twinkle in his eye, "She will come to guide you."

CHAPTER IV

Life After Death

And so I learned to meditate, and began to devote time regularly, morning and evening, to doing so. The ability of my mind to focus increased steadily, and I was able to sit for longer periods silently. Because I kept coming back to my meditation at regular hours, a continuity between the sessions grew, and the beginning of one session seemed to take up from the end of the last. During the times in between, as I went through the normal activities of my life, I felt a deeper focus, a very sensitive kind of attention, and a growing insight and ability to see deeply into the solution of even everyday problems.

The focus of my efforts was always the one great problem: why had the good woman, my mother, had to suffer and die; what force was it that came to every good and pure thing in the world—every joy, every relationship, every accomplishment—and with time inevitably tore it down, turned it to pain, wiped away its very existence. I felt that, if I could find this force, for surely there must be a cause behind the aging and death of all things, then perhaps I could change this cause, and change its seemingly inevitable effects.

In a more selfish and personal way, even with time, I still greatly missed my mother, thought of her often, wondered if she still existed in some way, if she were lost or needed help, if giving such help were possible, and how I would ever know. Again I was drawn to the Garden, where it seemed that, with time and my growth within, the answer to every question might be found.

I came to that blessed place as usual, in the dead of night, when the desert was quiet but for the soft and fragrant breezes—the scent of oleander from the Garden on the inside, planted by man; and the fainter but more pervasive smell of mesquite, planted by no man, floating in toward the Garden from the outside, from the desert.

I paused at the gate, where in earlier days I would have stood and watched for Her, waiting. But now it occurred to me to try another way to find Her, to draw Her into the Garden from within myself. And so I entered, walked to the great carob tree whose branches had been the only blanket between us and the stars, and sat again on the simple wooden bench there.

I bent over, put my head in my hands, and simply listened for Her. I placed myself into the quietness that Kamala Shila had taught me, and simply listened, between the rush of my own blood flow and breath sounds, between the great drum of the heartbeat sounds—as if by the act of listening, She would be compelled to return here.

My mind was empty and silent and tuned to one thing only—it is the way She walks, and the sound of Her footsteps; She walks not with a regular cadence but with a skip, as if always dancing, even when walking, and this I listened for, and waited only for that sound, my eyes closed. And there was a long waiting, and still nothing.

Then finally the silence of my mind was broken with a rustling, and very slow and stately footsteps, purposeful, and reflecting the purposefulness of the one who walked from the gate, behind me in the dark. I turned, and in the moonlight saw the master, Dharma Kirti.

The first thing his face told was but kindness, with sad wistful brown eyes, and a gentle, almost sad smile. The second impression was of a stateliness, the even stride of a nobleman, back and neck erect like a soldier, every movement speaking of decisiveness. And the final message was of sternness, a severity in the straight roman nose, the strongness of the chin, and above all the embers of intelligence and righteousness and fearlessness glowing behind the eyes. He stood silent, eyes fixed on mine for a minute or more, and then spoke—

"Come walk with me, in the Garden."

I rose; we started off to the left, past the low stone chapel, toward the lines of palms to the south.

"Is there something you wanted to speak about?" he asked, as we walked in the half shadows.

My heart as often was upon death, the death of my mother, wondering if she still was, somewhere. And along with this concern, honestly, there were two more; I thought as well of my own death, hardly able to imagine it, wondering if it would really happen, what would happen afterward—and then most importantly whether She would be with me as I died, and whether we would be together, after that.

"Is it true that we live on after we die, and that we have lived before we came here to this life?"

"Let me ask you questions, and perhaps you will have the answers," he replied, in a voice that was both soft in concern for my own concerns, as if he knew them perfectly, and yet also had an extra sound, one that led me to understand the iron hardness of the logic behind his words, the iron jaws of cold and inescapable reason, with which he had—in his life in India, thirteen centuries ago—challenged and defeated the unclear thinking of others.

"Please, if you would."

"What is the body made of?"

"Skin, blood, fluids, hard bones, softer organs, hair in some places to cover things."

"Are these things physical?"

"Yes, of course, we can touch them and feel them, press against them, they have weight, they can break or split; we even cut them open, when the need is great enough."

"And what is the mind made of?"

"I don't know if we in our times here would say *made of,* it's more just there, and filled sometimes more and sometimes less with thoughts, and wishes and hopes, which I listen to as they pass through that place, my mind."

"And are these thoughts like the parts of your body? Can you see them, or touch them, or break them into pieces?"

"If you mean, do they have color, or can they be hard or soft to touch, or warm or cold, or caress my hand like the water of the sea—no, not like that, just clear, and invisible, like crystal, like the air itself, weightless but moving on, in a steady stream, through my lifetime."

"But does your mind have a place of its own, where it stays, in the way that your arms and legs and head take up a certain place?"

"Well, they say it does have a place, in the head, under the bone, in something we call the brain . . ." My voice trailed off, for I had felt him start, his body twitching just slightly, and his face turned toward me, and the eyes fixed on me, and they began to burn, just slightly, like a wild animal that was asleep and now beginning to wake, dangerously.

"And the mind is in the brain?" he asked sternly.

"Yes, I think so."

"And not in your hand?" he said, suddenly grasping my hand in both his own—and I felt the power in his arms.

"Well, perhaps . . ." I was losing my confidence.

"So you do not feel my fingers?" But I did, more and more uncomfortably.

"Of course I do."

"So you are aware, in your hand?"

"Yes, yes, I am aware and I feel your hand."

"So your consciousness extends to your hand?"

"Yes," beginning to feel more sure of myself.

"So your mind extends to your hand?"

"Yes, yes, my mind, my consciousness, reaches all over my body, to the very edges of my skin, everywhere."

"So we can say that your mind is located everywhere within the confines of your skin?"

"Yes, yes, we can say that."

"And no farther?" Again, the steel glint in the eye, fixed on mine.

"No, no farther—I cannot feel beyond the ends of my fingers, I am not conscious beyond the ends of my physical body."

"So you cannot think of . . . that soft grass, back near the carob tree, just before the fountain?" he asked a little mischievously, as if he knew I thought often of that tender bed.

"Of course I can."

"Then we can say that your mind extends there too, out beyond the ends of your fingers, all the way back across the Garden?"

"Yes, yes, we can say that."

"So really the mind is ineffable, and far-reaching, and it can go far out beyond the limits of the physical body?"

"Yes."

"And in fact it is quite different from the body—it can fly to distant places, it can think of places far beyond the stars that look down upon us now?"

"Yes."

"And it is almost nothing like the body, this crystal bird of mind, it is not confined to this hard flesh and bone, it cannot be touched, it cannot be pressed against, it cannot be weighed, it cannot be seen or cut or measured, am I right?"

"Yes, all right."

"And so how can you say it is the brain, or that it is restricted to the brain, or that it lies in the brain, when it flies, at will, to all places?"

I began to feel even more uncomfortable, not the least because now my hand was completely wrapped in both of his, and clasped tightly against his chest, as his arguments increased in their intensity. "I didn't say the mind was the brain, I said it stayed in the brain."

"So mind and brain are related, the mind stays around the brain, and in fact around all the rest of your body too?"

"Yes, that's true."

"And do you agree that, when we say two things are related, it means they are separate things?"

"Yes, if two things are related, they must necessarily be two different things—every schoolboy monk knows that."

"So can we agree that the mind and body, although related, are two completely different things, different stuff altogether?"

"Yes."

"Now let me ask you something else," he said, and his stance changed, as he still clasped my hand, but the left foot out a bit toward me; and I knew that powerful arguments would be coming now, for this was the stance of the ancient debaters of India, as they stood and thundered at their opponents, pointing their body sideways, like a boxer, as if to provide less of a target for the blows that might be returned.

"Does the body change?"

"Of course, people get older, the body gets older, more wrinkles, less strength, gray hair."

"And why does the body change?"

"Many reasons, but the main one of course—any novice monk has learned this long ago—is that its causes change. As the causes change, the result changes. As the energy that produced the body wears out, then the body itself wears out, must wear out."

"And so if a thing changes, then this proves that the thing had a cause?"

"Yes."

"And what causes the body?"

"It has many causes, but I suppose the main one is the parents—the blood and egg of the mother, and the sperm of the father. When these two causes come together, and all the other contributing factors are present, then the body begins to grow, cell by cell."

"Yes, right, the physical parts of your mother and father came together, and your body began to grow. This is what we call the 'material' cause—the stuff that turned into the first moments of your body, in the same way that clay is the main cause, the material cause, for a ceramic dish. And with a dish too other factors must be present, such as a potter's hands and skill, and the oven to fire the clay, and time for the clay to cure. Material cause—you should understand material cause. What is the material cause for a tree?"

"I suppose the seed of the tree."

"Right. And the contributing factors?"

"The soil, the light of the sun, water, and careful tending."

"Right—so what makes the material cause different from the other factors?"

"As you said, I guess—it is the stuff that turns into the result; the essence that, when the right moment comes, flops over into the result—the seed is the stuff that at the right moment transforms into the sprout of the tree, and the clay is the stuff that transforms into the dish."

"And this stuff—the material of the cause—does it have to be similar to the material or stuff in the result?"

"Yes, I suppose so. In fact, they should have a lot in common, very similar to each other."

"So now we have reached the main point," said Master

Dharma Kirti, and indeed he had been moving me now I realized toward the darkest part of the Garden, in the shadows of the palms and the high southern wall, away from the moonlight, to a place where She and I had never in fact ventured. "Close your eyes," he said.

I closed them with a slight smile, thinking that in this dark corner of the Garden, it hardly mattered whether they were opened or closed. He opened my hand, still in his, and pressed it flat to his chest—and his ember eyes closed, and I could feel him go into meditation. It felt as though he were opening a channel or passageway from his heart to my mind, from his chest to my hand, and he spoke again—

"Picture your mind, over the length of your life, a clear crystal river of invisible stuff, flowing through the days that you have stayed in this world."

We were silent for minutes; I began to see the picture, a steady and connected flow of thoughts, stretching back to my earliest memories.

"Think of your mind as it was this afternoon, before you came to the Garden."

This I did.

"What was the material cause of your mind this afternoon? What was it that reached up to the first moment of your mind this afternoon, and then turned into your mind?"

I could see it clearly; no answer was needed, or expected. It was the mind, my own mind, from earlier the same day. My mind in the afternoon was the water of my mind in the morning, come downstream.

"Look again; see again—what was the material cause of this other mind: the mind you had this morning?"

Again I checked, and saw it was the mind of the previous evening, up until the time I awoke.

"And where did this year's mind come from?"

Last year's, of course, the clear river farther back.

"And where did last year's mind come from?"

The year before.

"And those of all the years before?"

From my own mind as a child, from a child's mind.

"And the child's mind?"

From the infant's mind.

"And the infant's mind?"

From the mind of the fetus, growing in the womb.

"There—catch it—put your mind on that. Think of a single tiny spot in the invisible river of the history of your mind—put your mind upon that very first moment of awareness, that very first instant of consciousness, however primitive, within the womb of your own mother."

Of course I could not remember it, but I could imagine it—it must have been there, my very first thought, my very first primitive awareness, I suppose some awareness of the warmth and moisture of my mother, of her presence surrounding me.

"Stop, hold that instant—focus all your mind on that first instant."

I did. He was silent. He was glaring at me, not with his eyes, but with his powerful mind. We broke into speech again.

"Did that first instant of thought ever change?"

"Of course, for I am thinking now, many years later."

"So did it have a cause?"

"Necessarily."

"Did it have a material cause?"

"Yes."

"Was the material cause of your very first thought something physical; something you could touch, or press against, or weigh, or cut?"

"No, no, we have already said that—the material cause has to be some similar stuff, the stuff of mind, and not the stuff of body."

"Another mind?"

"Of course."

"Whose?"

"My parents'?"

"Do you think like your parents?"

"In what sense?"

"Do you have their likes and dislikes, their insights, their doubts?"

"Some I share, but nothing like the same."

"You have a different state of mind?"

"Yes, my own, my mind has its own special likes and dislikes, and all the rest, ever since I was very young."

"So if it was not your parents' minds that caused this first moment of your mind, this first moment of awareness in the womb, then whose mind was it?"

"My own?"

"From where?"

"From before." He let my hand go, it slipped to my side, our eyes opened, his eyes on mine, with an intense look, almost like fury, a kind of divine exultation.

I saw that I had lived before, before I came to my mother.

"Good," he nodded, and his face began to soften again, and the ember died down. He was back to the quiet older monk, white-haired, with an age no one could decide, maybe forty, or fifty, or sixty, or ageless. "Good, good. You have seen it. And now you are really ready to learn something." He moved off toward the stronger light of the eastern wall of the Garden, where the water from the fountain laughs down in its quiet way, pulling me gently after him.

CHAPTER V

Death's Journey

I knew, from the words I had passed with Dharma Kirti, that my mother did still live—not because I had seen her with my eyes, but because I had seen her with my mind; and not because I could see her in my mind's eye, but because I could prove in my mind that she still existed; and this, I knew, gave the same truth as seeing with the eyes. My own fate too I felt was wrapped with hers; wherever she had gone, I should go too, this I felt was our bond. And wherever I went, I wanted a way to find the Golden One there as well.

I used the meditation as best I could, and sought to know these things, but it could not be done without help, and I almost knew it would be so. I resolved to return once more to the Garden—it was no difficult resolve, for this had always been the place of answers, and joy.

The season this time was winter, and the journey had kept me from arriving until quite late; I entered the gate near midnight. The moon this time was not full, but only a sliver, and a silver sheen of desert frost lay across the grass. The cold cut my body, and my patience, and I sat for the first time on the bench beneath the carob not with my back to the gate, but facing it—almost demanding that, for once, She come quickly. But I waited long, and it was only the last but strong threads of my faith that kept my eyes fixed upon the iron spikes atop the gate, where I must see the face of anyone approaching.

When he came I was startled—it was no golden face and hair, no light of the sun and warmth, but rather a bare skull, two dark sockets sunk in shadows of pale white, high above the gate. He crossed the ground from the gate to my bench softly and speedily, a specter, his robes trailing on the ground, accentuating his great height. Then he was beside me, staring down at me with his joyless face, the master of higher knowledge, Vasu Bandhu himself.

He was gaunt, and every limb long but not thin, rather strong and determined, with the stringy tendons of tenacity even at his age, which I guessed to be around seventy. His forehead was short, and his jaw square, everything taut and stretched, so that his skin seemed merely paint upon a skull. His lips were pursed, tightly, and etched into his cheeks at the ends of his lips were deep lines of deadly seriousness. I could not speak, and waited for his words; he continued to stand before me, staring down, and the soft grass and happy fountain were no longer with me, but behind me.

"Will you die today?" he asked simply.

From anyone else who looked like this, in this darkness and this loneliness, I might have taken his words almost as a threat—but the robes I trusted, the robes of a monk, and I answered just as simply, "I don't know."

"But think, *will you die today?*" he demanded.

"I could, it's always possible, there is always a chance . . . but it has not happened yet, and so I tend to think no, not today."

"Look at your body," he commanded. "Is this a body that will die?"

I stared down at my hands, and looked at the fingers, almost immobile in the cold, and thought of the hands of my mother's corpse, that morning when we found her deep in a pool of her own blood, when the cancers had eaten through to the heart itself—"Yes, yes, this is a body that will die."

"And when Death comes," he continued intensely, "is there someplace where you can go, is there any place that you know of, where Death cannot reach you?"

"No, no such place. No great stone castle, no boat on the sea, no hermitage deep in a forest, no iron chamber. Death reaches into any of them, unstoppable."

"But you are young. Isn't death for the old? Does not Death take his victims in a logical order, from the oldest first, and then those younger?"

I thought for a moment. "We must certainly die, and so we look more for death among those who have lived long; but no, I cannot say that there is any sure order, it seems almost random, and many of my young friends have died as well—Death seems to respect no order."

"But surely there must be some means of stopping Death,

some new advance in the practice of medicine, some sacred incantations known to some high priests, some way of concealing our life from Death."

"Oh, there are medicines, and sometimes they seem to slow his coming; but no, no doctor yet has found any medicine to actually stop Death, and no priest has found any words that can keep his hands away."

"But these medicines, could we not use them wisely, and expend the best efforts and talents of our people, to find healthful ways of eating, and exercising the body, and thus find a way to add to the hours of our life?"

I thought carefully, for this same question had come to me frequently, and the answer had disquieted me. "Yes, we can do all these things, and it would seem that it should add to the time of our life—but paradoxically, even during the time that we exercise, and even during the hours that we seek out healthful foods, and cook and eat them—even as we do these things, those same hours have leaked away, inexorably, and swept us still closer to our death. The time that we take to live is time that is lost to life, and time that always, forever, takes us still closer to death. We cannot stop, we cannot slow, the race to die."

Vasu Bandhu stood silent, and as the sound of my own words subsided in my ears, I heard the spring, flowing from the fountain behind me, and it felt as though he were beckoning me to think of the water, my life, seeming to be one solid thing, a spring between the rocks, but in reality a continual leaking away, flying away, of precious moments, without a pause.

"And how many hours did you meditate today?" he asked finally.

"Well, normally I am quite regular, but today I had extra work to do at the library, and there was the preparation for the trip here, and then a quick dinner at the inn, and . . ."

"Answer the question."

"I did not meditate at all, there was no time."

"And yesterday, when you did have time. How long did you meditate? How long did you devote to the greater quest, how much time did you give to your spirit, instead of that body, so soon as it is to rot?"

"Oh, yesterday I did meditate, nearly an hour, in the morning."

"A single hour in an entire day?" he asked.

"Well, I usually try to meditate for an hour, some in the morning, some in the evening."

"A single hour?" he repeated.

"Well, that's including the preparation and all; and oftentimes there is some work to prepare for the day, or some interruption from outside my chambers. I suppose honestly it is more like half an hour, or perhaps twenty minutes."

"Twenty minutes, in a day of twenty-four hours?" he asked again.

"Yes, yes, total I think about twenty minutes, when I can." I looked down at the cold ground.

"And eating, how much time eating?" he asked. "And sleeping, and talking with your friends, and thinking thoughtlessly about what you might have done, or might still do. And even defecating; how much time?"

"Well, all those—this is how the day goes, this is how I pass the day."

"So really it is as though you have died already; there is so little, so little precious time before death, and really this little time itself is wasted, and so really there is no time at all. You have no time at all. You are I would say as good as dead already."

I sat silent.

"Do you know," he asked gently, as if from experience, "what the life behind him looks like to a man of seventy years?"

"No, I am still young."

He sighed. "Imagine a long dream, a dream like life itself, filled sometimes with pleasant experiences, disfigured by moments of great pain, but full and colorful nonetheless."

I could imagine it.

"And imagine now the moment of waking."

This too I imagined.

"And imagine now the feeling of a person, who has just woken, as he looks back upon the dream."

I did, for I had dreamt such dreams, and it struck me only that the entire dream seemed like a few moments, quickly drifting away. He nodded, and stood silent for a while, and then, once more, "I asked you—will you die today?"

"I really don't know," I said honestly.

"Then let me tell you a story," he said quietly, his voice rasping. "There is a man. He has done some great wrong to another man, a very strong and dangerous man. And the dangerous man has threatened the first man, and he has sworn to him, that before the month is over, he will come to his house at night, and break in, and cut his throat."

I shivered slightly at his words, and at the night cold, and at the whole feeling that had descended upon my cherished Garden.

"Now I ask you; if there are preparations to be made—if there are locks to be put on the doors, and bolts on the shutters, and ways worked out to call for help when the moment arrives—

is it better if the first man made these preparations on the eve of the first night, or should he wait for the next night, or five nights hence, knowing that the man with the knife would come on some night, on any night, ere the end of the month?"

"Well, of course, he should make his preparations immediately."

"But what if the man with the knife comes later, perhaps even on the last night of the month, or the night before that?"

"Well, no matter, for the preparations have already been made; but if the preparations were made later, and the murderer arrived earlier, then all would be lost."

"You are right, of course. What is the length of a human life?"

"In these days, seventy years. People live to seventy."

"No, no, I did not ask the average *span* of life. I asked, What is the length of a human life? How long does a person live?"

"Well, some live longer, and some less. Most nowadays live to about seventy."

He cleared his throat, and his eyes shifted away, in near anger. "I ask you again, What is the length of a human life?"

"Well, if you put it that way . . ."

"What way?" he retorted.

"Well, all right. I cannot say, we do not know, there is no fixed length to the life of a human. Life has no definite length—some die in their old age, others in the richness of middle age, others in the bloom of youth, others as infants, others even before they have left the womb. There is no certain number of days to our life, to anyone's life."

"And is it easy to die, or difficult to die?" he continued, relentlessly.

"I feel it must be somewhat difficult; I have been alive now over twenty years, more even than a sturdy wagon, nearly half the life of a desert house built of stone and mortar."

"So you have never seen or heard of a man who died from a small cut that got infected, or from slipping in a small pool of water, or from the sudden blow of a fist, struck in a moment of anger?"

"Well, yes, I have heard or seen all of them."

"And you have never seen or heard of a man who was killed by the very things that are supposed to keep us alive: never knew of someone who was crushed by a wagon or had his skull smashed by the kick of a milk cow; someone who choked on some delicious dish his wife had just carefully cooked; someone who died in the hands of a doctor administering his treatments; someone who fell down the stairs of his house, or who died when a brick or piece of the roof that was supposed to shelter him killed him?"

"Just so, it happens often, I think."

"And you have studied some physiology; tell me, what is the function of the lungs?"

"To cool the body, to supply air, and to moderate the influence of the hotter element, of bile."

"And what is the function of the liver?"

"To produce bile, to aid in digestion, so that food can fuel and warm the body."

"And if the warmth of the body is insufficient, if the wind element around the lungs becomes too strong?"

"A man dies of pneumonia."

"But if the wind element itself weakens, and there is no cooling of the body?"

"Then a man dies of fever."

"So can we say that our own body, this machine that seems to be in such wonderful balance within itself, is really a fatal accident waiting to happen; that the functions of the very organs within the body place these organs at war against each other, and that it is merely a matter of time until one organ dominates the others and kills this body off?"

It was strange to think that, if nothing outside of me killed me, my own body would do so, but I had to admit it was true. "Thus it is."

"And so isn't it true to say that this body is killed very easily? Isn't it true to say that, as we surround ourselves with things to shelter and feed and transport and comfort us, it is these very objects, or in fact the body itself, that most likely will kill us?"

I was becoming increasingly uncomfortable thinking about things that we naturally prefer to leave unthought, but I had to agree, and nodded silently.

"And isn't it true further that it is nearly an impossibility, and an activity which consumes almost an entire lifetime, simply to provide for the physical needs of this body? Do not most of the men and women around this planet work their entire day simply to feed and clothe themselves, and do they not frequently fail in this task and die from want?"

"Yes, all true, all true."

"We are then, you must admit, literally born to die, am I right?"

I nodded again.

Vasu Bandhu was silent again, and the entire Garden took on a great silence, not at all like the joyful silence of the master Kamala Shila within his meditation, but rather a silence like death, a winter silence, and the Garden seemed as though it were made entirely of the stone of the walls, and not of the vitality of its lovely plants and trees.

I turned my eyes up to him again; he was looking away, at the darkness above the southern wall to his right, lost in thought. And then he looked down again at me, and I was struck by the metamorphosis of his face: the stone cold had turned to an almost burning compassion, and his eyes were bright, brimming with tears.

"And if a man has family, and friends—loved ones, close companions, lifetime companions, wife and children and comrades who have walked with him through an entire life—then when this man dies, when this man is dying, lying on his bed, and dying in that hour, then do they come, and stand, surrounding him, weeping, with some grasping his hands, and others stretching their hands out to touch his cheek or breast or legs?"

"Yes, yes, I have seen it myself, I have been there at the bedside myself."

"And have you seen how, even as they clutch at him, he passes on?"

"Yes, seen."

"Passes on, alone?"

"Yes, alone; the others can be holding him, but none can go along."

"But surely, even if no one can go with him, he can pick up and take together with him a few of the things that are dear to him, just a few of the objects for which he has consumed an entire lifetime, working to gather them together, striving to secure them within the confines of the house he calls his own?"

"No, no, an entire lifetime wasted, every object, every single piece of every object, every penny, every possession, every hard-won bit of everything he ever owned, left behind, totally."

"But the body? Even the precious and most cherished body? Even the body, our own body, which we fed so carefully, so many years; which we clothed with care, for warmth and beauty; the hair that we daily arranged into various styles, the skin that we bathed and oiled to maintain, our own face, our very identity?"

"No, nothing, not our body, not even our name. We can take nothing; we are utterly, entirely alone."

"And at this moment, in the final moment, who do they call to come and help? Is there some close friend who can assist us, is there some powerful authority or wealthy patron who can be summoned, is there a doctor who at the very moment of death can be looked upon for help?"

"No, none, it is useless. There is no one to call; no one left to call, no one is called."

"And so we can say, in conclusion, that it is absolutely certain that we must die?"

"Yes."

I could hardly bear to look up at him. "Yes, this is what they say."

He glared at me furiously, like a man who had just found out a traitor, a traitor whose lies had caused the pain and death of many innocent people. "And can you give me," he demanded, "a single shred of proof that the mind dies when the body dies?"

"Well, when the body dies, the person stops moving, and stops talking, and seems to stop thinking as well."

"And can you see this, do you know, that he has stopped thinking?"

"No, we cannot see the mind, it is not like the body, it is not made of the same stuff as the body; it is something invisible, and knowing, and nothing like the skin and bone, which can be touched, and cut, and measured. But we can guess what the mind is thinking from the expressions and sounds that come from the face of the body."

"And so you are saying that when the body has broken down, beyond repair—when the ability of the body to move the tongue and facial expressions has ended—then this invisible and knowing thing called mind has ended, simply because it can no longer be expressed in the face and words?"

I saw what he was getting at: it was as if to say that a person riding a horse must be dead simply because the horse was dead; that the hand holding a hammer must be dead when only the handle of the hammer was broken. It began to dawn on me that this idea, the idea that the invisible and ineffable mind must die when the tool through which it expressed itself died, was only one of those things we believe because our parents believed it; that it was only one of those unexamined concepts which we believe because all those around us believe it, and have believed it since we were children; and that our children too will believe it only because we do, for absolutely no good reason at all. I did not have a single proof to give to Vasu Bandhu that the mind should die only because the body died and we could no longer then see the influence of this mind upon the body.

"I know you have seen, with the infallible eyes of reason, that you lived before; you may not know the details, and I am not claiming that you can know them, easily, but you know, through cold logic, divorced from the indefensible assumptions by which we are surrounded as children, that you have lived before. And so it is entirely logical that your mind should continue, and that it does not break down simply because the body breaks down."

"Suppose it does," I said, somewhat hopefully, since we had finally reached the point for which I had journeyed to the Garden—to find some news of my mother, and of my own future, future with Her.

"Then naturally it must go somewhere," he stated simply.

"Oh yes," I said, "I have heard them talk about it; about reincarnation; and how we must find the person who exists now, who was in the past our loved one, and some people seek out seers, people who can tell where our loved ones have gone." I looked up at Vasu Bandhu, to see if his wisdom could guide me.

He looked directly into my eyes, and this time the tears were flowing freely down the hard face, and the raspy voice choked with emotion. "Do you imagine," he asked softly, "that a human life, the kind of life you now live, and your mother did live, is easily found? Do you suppose that every mind that goes on, goes on to such a body and life?"

"Well, that's what they say," I answered insistently, not wanting to hear what I suspected I might now hear from him.

He looked away again, and then back. "Do you really imagine, if you think about it even for a moment, that the world you see before you now is the only world; can you really imagine, being a normal thinking person, that every possible realm, where any possible form of life exists, is here before your eyes? Does not the fact of the world you see here itself suggest to you that there are other worlds, and in fact quite probably a nearly endless number of other worlds, of which you have no awareness?"

Thinking even for a brief moment, and catching sight of the stars in the cold air over his shoulder, and thinking of microcosms of beings that existed seen and unseen within the very grass and spring of the Garden, and reflecting on the endless chambers of my own mind, those places in it that were familiar to me, and those I knew I had not yet even discovered—I had to admit that the world I knew was probably only the most infinite sliver of a vastly greater universe of infinitely varied realms. And close on the heels of this thought came another, a complete despair, of ever finding my mother again.

He sensed my thoughts, and spoke softly but insistently. "I will tell you briefly of the realms; you need not believe me now, but these things can be proven, and they will be proven to you when the time comes; and they can be seen, and you can see them yourself as well—I should say, you *will* see them—when that time comes in turn.

"There are realms, there are realms to which the mind goes, where when you first open your eyes you are in the grown body of a person. And when you look up, the first thing that you see is another person, and they are carrying a knife or a club, and they are coming at you in fury. You instinctively reach around on the ground; you grasp at anything, a stick, a stone, and you snatch it up, and you are driven by something inside you to attack as well—and so you live, an entire life, simply in the fury of killing, striving to kill all around you, or be killed. And if you are killed, you suffer from a peculiar curse, that you cannot die, and must rise again within minutes, to struggle and suffer, over and over, for thousands of years.

"There are realms where, when you open your eyes, you are simply covered in fire. You cannot die. You burn. You feel the agony of burning. You scream, and scream, and only scream, and there is nothing else to do, nothing that can be done. You burn.

"There are realms of running, only running, running to escape great terrible dogs, with iron fangs that rip and tear at your legs, and nowhere to go, and no end, just running.

"There are realms of constant want, there are realms of spirits, driven by hunger and thirst, moaning and wandering and searching for comfort they can never find, but searching still, endlessly, hopelessly. These are realms that you cannot now see."

He paused, and looked away again, and I was aware for the first time that my own face was wet, from tears that had dropped from his.

"Even this world, even the realms you can see . . ." he said quietly. "Imagine what it is to be an animal here in this realm. I know you people, I know your thoughts, you imagine that the animals live in some kind of natural harmony, some kind of communing with the trees and waters and mountains. But let me tell you what it is really like, and you stop me if I speak wrong. Why do you imagine that the birds start and fly when you approach? Why do you think the fish dart away when the shadow of a human hand crosses the surface of their water? Why did you ever think the deer ran from you, and the fox and raven and mouse; why always running from you, in terror?

"It is because the life of an animal is a life of terror; the life of an animal is only one thing, only one activity, and that is to escape becoming the food of other animals. Animals are either eating or being eaten. They eat the less powerful, they are eaten by the more powerful. They run because they do not want to be eaten. They spend an entire existence looking over their shoulder for danger, and you are the danger. You are a more powerful animal. You are the ultimate danger. You are the animal that will catch them, and force them to do your work, or strip them of their skin for your clothing, or eat their flesh for your food.

"Know then, really, what it is to be an animal. Know what even the realms you can see are really like. And do not," he said almost angrily, "do not imagine, do not deceive yourself, into thinking that, if any mind can take this form of life, your own mind could never take this form of life. Do not be so arrogant, do not be so unthinking. Use your mind, realize that your mind goes on, realize that it must go somewhere, realize that other minds have gone to these realms, realize that your mind could, very well, go to these realms as well. The mind does not end. The mind cannot be stopped. You cannot stop your mind, even if you wished to, and it must go on, and there are realms beyond your imagination, realms of unthinkable suffering, where it may well go."

He stood at the end of these passionate words nearly breathless, and his age and the cold seemed to grip him for the first time, and he looked down at me, tired and sad.

"You must not go to these realms, I do not want you to go to these realms. We said before that nothing, no one, can help you at the moment of your death. But this is not so, for there is something which can help, and that is knowledge, sacred knowledge, knowledge of things spiritual. This knowledge you can learn, and will learn. For the time being, though, review what I have taught you, the three principles of death: that its coming is certain, that its time is uncertain, and that no worldly thing can help you then. Meditate upon each of the points we spoke of, to prove death's certainty, and all the rest, to yourself. This is what we call the meditation on death.

"I do not speak to worry you, it is not my wish to frighten

you. This is not the purpose of death meditation. A man who never learned this meditation, a man who never did this meditation, has cause—great cause—to fear death, and will at the moment of death be filled with terror. But if you learn this meditation, and master it, and then learn the preparations to be undertaken, then you can die with confidence, without any fear at all, for you have planned your journey; you know the path beyond, and the realm to which it leads—a good realm, a good place.

"The strong man with the knife will come, before the month ends, to murder his enemy. Lock the doors, prepare yourself; learn what must be learned, and begin—tonight."

CHAPTER VI

Freedom

The cold night with the master Vasu Bandhu left me shaken, and feeling even further from the answers I sought. If all he said were true, and I had no way in my own mind to disprove any of what he said, then I was faced not simply with a vague yearning to find and help my mother, and to understand what I felt was something very important spiritually with the Lady of the Garden; rather, the matter was much more urgent. If the mind did not stop at death—and as far as I could see there was absolutely no evidence that it did—and if there were a nearly infinite variety of worlds and forms of life into which my mind could wander after death; and if many of these forms of life, judging from the tears in Vasu Bandhu's eyes, were sheer suffering, then my leisurely quest had become more of a very deadly race against time, against my own death.

Thus my next trip to the Garden took place as soon as I could leave my affairs, in the early spring of the following year. This is the time of year when the desert is in a state of flux, not as in the lands where large trees and much greenery grow, and where the spring winds begin to awaken the branches, which then begin to push forth buds; the desert at this time is in the daytime a pleasing mix of warmth and cool, in the nighttime turning to a crisp but not unpleasant coolness, laced with the warmth of the day, and the vibrancy of the subtle pastel colors begins to deepen, notch by notch.

As I entered the gate of the Garden this time I had an instinct not to sit on the usual bench, but instead upon that cherished piece of grass, softer in this season with fresh thin shoots of fine green. I sat, pulled up my knees, and rested my chin upon them, looking at the crystal water as it spilled over the lip of the fountain, and eventually closing my eyes, dreaming rather than willing that She might finally come.

I heard no sound but in time felt something odd, a radiant warmth at my side, and then an exquisite fragrance which I can hardly describe, something like gardenia, or hibiscus, mixed with a kind of honey, and all of it again radiating an almost unearthly warmth. This was the closest thing to Herself that I had as an adult ever experienced in this place, and with a quiet prayer I cocked my head to the left, resting my right cheek on my knee, and opened my eyes, slowly.

Although I had never laid eyes upon such a being, or at least was not aware of it if I had, I knew at once this was Maitreya—the Enlightened One who, it is said, will come next to walk on this planet. I recognized his form from the old scroll paintings, which were painfully beautiful but did him no justice; I suppose that the painters must have frustrated themselves attempting to re-create his magnificence over the past sixteen centuries, since the last human had met him face-to-face and his Five Great Books had come to our lands.

He sat as I did, on the grass, with his knees bent before him, leaning back, every inch of his form proclaiming an absolute grace and ease. His hair was black and long, flowing over his shoulders, and he had a body of youthfulness, slender and muscled, glowing in a very soft and subtle golden light. He wore a blue loincloth of some shining, flowing material like silk, and was covered, in a glorious and unabashed innocence, with various jewels: long earrings of turquoise in gold, a choker on his neck of soft white diamonds, a breast piece of ruby and a kind of moonstone, fine armbands of gold filigree and sapphire, and loosely around his ankles chains of gold intertwined with strings of precious beads and pearls in rose, ebony, and ivory hues.

His face was strong and handsome, and unmistakably manly, while there was a magnetic feminine quality in the way he moved and sat, and so he seemed like a being who was complete in himself, a kind of living perfection. He looked at me with a frank expression of perfect love and compassion, as though I were at once his child, and lover, and wife and dearest brother; and there was mixed there a kind of deep concern, as though he had just learned that I was terribly ill, and had only little time left to live.

"I do love you" were his first words, spoken naturally, with perfect ease, as though this were the first thing a person should ever say to an absolute stranger, and mean it with total sincerity.

I smiled, and felt immediately in the presence of an old and dear friend, and we sat, simply looking into each other's eyes, without any need for words. Eventually, I do not know how long it was, he shifted, and fixed his gaze upon the rare lovely desert water flowing from the fountain. Then he spoke again.

"I know your mind, I know whatever has ever been in your mind, I know whatever will come to your mind, I know your mind now: I know your mind. But it would be a pleasure for me," he turned his eyes again to mine, slowly, "if we enjoyed together the pleasure of speaking, and so I ask you, dear one, to speak as will make you feel happiest, and I too will join with you."

I felt no hesitation, and no distance at all between us, a complete comfort to pour out all I had been thinking. And this I did, to the effect that I was frightened for my mother, for I knew she must still exist, and now knew she might be in grave danger. I felt lost as well myself, and was becoming increasingly less hopeful of finding what I was driven to find with Her, here in the Garden. He listened with perfect attention, again with that look, which at the moment felt to me like the look of a pure and innocent and loving child as he gazes up to the face of his mother.

"Above all things I want you to find what you seek; nothing would bring me more happiness," he said with a ring of perfect truth. "And so the last thing I would ever want to do is cause you more doubts, more concern. But I am bound to speak truthfully—I am not capable of doing otherwise—and I tell you: the realms of which Vasu Bandhu spoke, the terrors of these realms, are perhaps as nothing compared to the sufferings of your own realm, of your own world; the aura of suffering which surrounds you and those who live with you here, in your own world, is more difficult for those like me to look upon than all the sufferings of those other, hidden realms.

"Perhaps it is because you are so close to leaving all suffering, because you have within your reach all you need to reach total Freedom. Or perhaps," he said, his face suddenly distorted slightly, as though he were about to break into tears, "perhaps what is so difficult to watch is how you suffer, without realizing that you suffer, and so suffer so quietly, and constantly, and hopelessly."

"What are these sufferings, teach me these sufferings, so at least I may know the truth," I found myself saying, in a pleading voice, in the voice of a man asking to be told hard truths that he perhaps has always known, yet never dared to face.

He turned his golden face to me, and the loving deep brown eyes, and spoke gently: "In the world in which you live now, in the kind of life that you are forced to follow now, nothing is fixed. Have you not noticed? You can trust nothing, nothing stays the same. The forces that run your world, the forces that created your world and you yourself, and which dictate the very movement of time and events throughout your life, have a certain quality, a certain fluctuation, and so it is impossible that any one thing in your world will stay that way for you, for very long.

"And this hurts the most," he said with a soft sigh, "when you people finally find someone that you can love, in a way, and who loves you; and then the gears change, and the forces shift, and—despite yourselves, it is not your fault really, but driven by forces already set in motion—you both change, and the love changes to liking, and the liking merges into ignoring, and the ignoring descends into dislike, and finally the dislike into hatred, and so it happens, so often in your world, by the very nature of your world, that finally you come to hate that thing which first you loved, and those closest to you become the very ones for whom, in the end, you feel nothing."

The truth of his words, the confirmation lent to his words by my entire life, drew a kind of pain from me, and the pain radiated out, and away, toward him—where it was met halfway by that golden light, and I felt as if a parent were embracing a hurt child, and comforting him merely by his presence.

He paused, as if unwilling to continue, but I nodded silently, asking him without words to go on, as if we both knew I needed to know, so that I could be free, so that finally I could even want to be free.

He stared directly into my face, as if to hold me up with those loving eyes. "And there is another suffering you people have, which is the most cruel, and which I tell you of now only because I love you. In your present state you are all completely and totally incapable of the emotion of satisfaction, of contentment. Your desire is endless, and like some great scourge it drives you, whips you ahead of it mercilessly, drives you to get, to try to get, more and more, always more than what you have. You struggle, hopelessly, like small insects, to wrest some small and insignificant happiness away from the world, away from your fellow insects, and then—as soon as it is yours—your discontentment forces you to rise again, and race for a second small and insignificant happiness which, should you by some dumb luck acquire, cannot itself satisfy you either, and you are up and away again . . ." He paused, as if the very act of imagining how our minds worked was somehow painful for him.

"Imagine," he said, gazing through me this time, to some point in space behind me, "imagine what it feels like, to sit and observe, with a mind that knows all things, an infinite string of stars and planets, and upon an infinite number of those planets beings, and these infinite numbers of beings, as each planet turns daily to face its nearest star, awakening with the morning, and racing through the few precious hours of their lives, driven and beaten mercilessly by their dissatisfaction to scrounge for meaningless pleasures that are increasingly harder and harder to obtain, and simply impossible to maintain once obtained, and then to watch these poor beasts drop, the energy of their bodies and minds exhausted, and die from these futile efforts—all because they cannot be contented with what they already have, which in nearly every case is all they need to reach, as I have reached, true happiness."

And Maitreya stopped this time for a long time, for a pause that was cruelty itself, the most unintended cruelty from the being least inclined to anything but pure love, for I could not fail to see that he was describing my very life, and the life of all those around me.

Finally he stretched across the grass, moving luxuriously like a cat despite himself, and lifted a handful of sand from between the roots of the carob. He rolled over onto his stomach and stared into the grass, which was softly illumined by the light emanating from his face. He lifted the handful of sand slowly, dreamily, and then began to release a thin trickle; the grains flashed slightly as they fell through the light from his face, and began to collect in a tiny pile between several blades of grass.

"Look at the pile," he commanded me softly. "It is the size of a Himalayan peak, it is a mountain which blocks out half the sky, it dwarfs the imagination. And each grain of sand is a body, a separate corpse, some fat, some thin, some dark, some lighter, some with two legs, some with four, some young, others old, some covered with fur, some with the softest fairest flesh of a lovely infant; thousands and millions of corpses, piled here, between the blades of grass. These bodies are yours, for I have watched you, and waited, and hoped, century after century, that you would one day be pure enough to see me, and in those years, those many years, you have taken on one kind of body after another, endless bodies, myriad bodies, crawled in them, walked in them, flown with them, died with them, again and again, racing for nothing, through a lifetime of nothing, and dying with nothing." He leaned down and blew the pile away.

We were silent again for a moment, but I sensed he was not yet finished with this portrait of my existence, and he shifted again, again with that luxurious movement, and lay on his back, staring up at the starry night in an evident perfect happiness, reminding me of Her.

"Such stars, such high stars. Do you know, perhaps it would make you happy somehow to know, that as I have watched you over the course of the wakening and dying of entire galaxies, you have reached incredible heights. I have seen you raised up by the citizens of an entire planet to be their absolute emperor; I have seen you be the first and only human to climb the highest of mountains in your world; I have seen you be, by far, the most exquisitely beautiful woman, the most fabulously wealthy merchant, the most admired, most famous, most talented, most intelligent, and most acclaimed of all the beings upon your planet.

"And yet each time, and you know this from your own life, you slipped, things changed, you became a little less beautiful, or a little less quick, or a little less strong, and someone else was there, and merciless time dragged you down, until you were lower than when you began, worse than when you started, not only nothing, but a forgotten and neglected nothing. There is no position of fame, or happiness, or material well-being, or comfort of friends or family or home, which does not in time descend into the lowest condition of decay and, finally, simple dust. Believe me, for I have seen it, and you know it is true, as I do love you.

"And all this would be more bearable," he said with a tone of finality, "if we could go together; if we understood our suffering and banded together, as one, all living kind, to face our pains together, to love and support one another. But this again is not allowed by the forces which shape this existence; these powers shove us on through time, push us ahead of them through a short and violent life, and allow us only the briefest pause to be together with others. We pass through life, we connect with friends or lovers or spouses or family, find comfort and companionship and support one with the other, and then these forces rip us apart, inevitably. There is no one here in your realm with whom you can stay; there is no one who can walk with you more than an instant; and then you are thrown, inexorably, into a future of complete aloneness. You are always alone; you are born alone, you pass through this realm alone, and then you die, always, alone." He sighed, closed his eyes, and lay back against the grass, at total peace inwardly, at total despair of my life and world.

It seemed as though hours passed, and we lay on the grass, while I tried to grasp his words, difficult as it was, the saddest of worlds, described by the most contented of all beings. Then a light began gently to fill the space where we lay, until the entire area below the reaches of the carob tree was bathed in a soft golden aura. I remember thinking that dawn had come, and how tired I should have felt, though I did not, but then realized that Maitreya himself was now glowing, in an almost incandescent brightness, and providing a new sunlight for the plants and trees.

His eyes opened slowly, luxuriously, never more than half

open, reminding me of that One who had always seemed in some mysterious state of pleasure which was beyond me. He smiled broadly and whispered, "That question you were going to ask—please."

I felt a twinge of strangeness in attempting to speak to a being who knew everything I had ever said or would say, but I was truly overwhelmed by the most obvious of questions: "What, though, is the cause of all these things? What are these forces which you keep mentioning? Why must we suffer so? What drives us to suffer? Must it always be so?" I asked urgently.

Now he reached out, and sat up cross-legged, directly across from me; he took my hand in his lap, and unconsciously began to stroke it. I felt some embarrassment and lightly tried to pull my arm back, but his hands were strong, and I wondered a little at my own hesitation, thinking I could not love enough even to be loved by perfect love. He stroked my hand.

"Imagine," he said, and the light seemed to turn brighter by another degree, bathing my entire face and chest in warm gold. "Imagine what it would be like, if every time someone around you got something they wanted, you were overcome with perfect joy. Imagine if you felt as happy as they did as they received a word of praise, or were granted some prized and long-hoped-for object, or found a new and dear companion or friend. And imagine that you could feel this way even if you had been hoping to get that thing or person for yourself; imagine that you could share other people's happiness so perfectly that you could not distinguish it from your own. What I mean is, imagine what it would be like to live, the rest of your life, totally free of the emotion of..." he paused, as if searching for a word that he could not remember, because he had not even thought of it for centuries "... jealousy."

And with that he disengaged one of his hands from mine, and reached out, and with one of his fingers traced softly a line down the center of my forehead, starting from the top, and ending just above the point between my two eyebrows. With this soft touch I felt an emotion of extreme relief, of a great release from some great sorrow, and the skin on my forehead relaxed in a way that it had never done since jealousy, whose victim I had been since childhood, first carved its furrow there. I truly could imagine at that moment spending the rest of my days without jealousy, and it occurred to me how much time it would save me, how much of the limited space of my mind would be freed for other and happier thoughts; I felt as though someone had released me from some small closet, into a great golden room reserved only for the most graceful, quiet, and joyous dance.

"And now suppose," his entire visage was by now an even greater and more lovely smile, "that you understood totally the very most fundamental forces of reality itself, and so understood perfectly how to bring about the things you wish for, anything you could wish for, so that you never again needed to struggle blindly, reaching and grasping for things, but could simply wait knowingly and contentedly for the certain results of your own goodness. What I am trying to say, and it is somewhat hard for me to express it to you in a way that you can understand, is this: what if you were totally free of that emotion which troubles you creatures so much, the emotion which makes you so unhappy, and unfulfilled—what if you no longer," he paused again, to find words again, "wanted things?"

This idea was infinitely more difficult for me, but I felt immediately, perhaps more through the caress of his hand than by his words, exactly what he meant. He was not talking of any kind of wanting at all—I sensed for example that he wanted me to understand, and that he wanted me to be happy—but he was speaking rather of that sort of wanting which on a daily basis, on a moment-by-moment basis, upset my heart, ruined my peace, prevented me forcefully from the very feelings of satisfaction and happiness which wanting itself was supposed to fulfill. I had just a brief taste then of that feeling of which he spoke, and I went from the room of the dance to a pale blue sky: my mind was as free and wide as this sky itself, and when I thought of my life ahead it seemed as though it could be nothing but quiet and certain happiness. I barely felt his palm, flat on my forehead, like a mother pressing a cool, damp, and soothing cloth upon the cheek of a feverish child.

"And the opposite," he said next, and his voice sounded now like all the birds of the Garden, as the Sun approached with the end of night. "Picture yourself now, and see something happening, or someone coming, that is unpleasant: picture such an event, picture such a person. Something not going as planned. Someone saying something harsh to you. Yourself unable to get something you need. And now imagine that you respond with perfect equanimity; you understand exactly the ultimate causes for these events, you know what makes them, you know how they will end, and for the moment you simply watch them, with sadness perhaps, but not with that emotion you call . . . dislike."

Again I was made aware of the vast gap between the way this golden being thought and the ways in which I could think. I tried to picture how I would be if I had no dislike of anything at all; and again I knew instinctively the more precise meaning of his words, I knew that he in his enlightened way disliked the fact that I and all those around me were suffering, but I knew that his dislike was more a form of compassion, that his concern for us could only feel sweet and healthy in his heart, and that he was incapable of the confusion and hurt which we felt when we disliked some irritating person, or some unwanted circumstance in our life.

It was clear to me that he was not saying, "Imagine what it would be like not to feel pain," or "Imagine what it would be like if you didn't care that you were feeling pain," but rather, "Imagine what it would be like if, when pain came to you, you saw perfectly the causes deep within reality itself which were bringing this to you, and had a deep and well-founded peace of mind, as you went joyfully about the business of finishing this and other such pain forever."

And indeed this thought released my mind further, as if now it could fly off from the blue into the stars of the sky; imagine, an entire lifetime ahead of me, my mind freed completely of those thoughts and emotions which made it such an unhappy place to live, and so much free space now, so much free time within the mind itself, to love, to create, and to give to others. I found myself staring up at the boughs of the carob, transported, transfixed, and unaware even of Maitreya himself.

"Wait a bit," he laughed softly, delighted with my delight, "it is even better." And I placed my eyes and heart in his again.

"Imagine with me now," he smiled, "a world in which you are just a child, an innocent, laughing, expectant, happy child. You walk through life open and willing, happy to learn from everyone around you. Every time you meet someone, you find in them something you can learn, some sweet and precious lesson—you know how to listen carefully, as if for the sound of a single songbird in the desert, and unfailingly you are granted some diamond or ruby of understanding, which fills still further your already overflowing heart. Everyone is your dear teacher, everyone is giving you some jewel for your life. Again, I hardly know how to say it in words which you grasp, but what I mean is—imagine yourself, think of your own mind, for the rest of your entire life, cleansed completely of the emotion of—what do you call it now?" He looked at me mischievously, as if I were supposed to guess the word, but its opposite as he described it was so unfamiliar to me that I found myself at a loss, and so finally he filled it in: "Pride."

I could not honestly hope that I could overcome this dear and constant companion, but I did grasp the idea of the openness of the child, and this thought felt like some precious gift which perhaps I could uncover myself someday in the future, hidden away somewhere along the path of my life. Maitreya was infectious. I was feeling, well, happy.

"Now close your eyes," he continued, and I felt the warm tips of his fingers lightly on my face and eyelids, "and pretend that you have come to a perfect understanding of the very keys of existence: nothing is a mystery to you, you know the real causes behind every event, you know the deep and hidden connections between all existing things, you know what people have sought to know for the entire existence of all worlds, you know why every thing that ever happens happens, you know why every thought is thought, you know why every pain is felt, and you know the perfect solution to every pain—or rather, you understand perfectly the guiding principles that really move all the realms, and no event is to you unexplainable, no problem without its solution.

"In short, you know exactly how to act in order to achieve both daily and ultimate happiness, for yourself and all around you. Your mind is completely free of the emotion . . . what shall we call it? It is the great failure of all living kind to understand life itself, it is the state of mind that thinks one must take, and not give, in order to receive; it is the state of mind that thinks one must satisfy oneself, and not others, in order to be truly happy; it is that total misunderstanding of how things are which drives men to destroy, methodically and thoroughly, throughout the length of their entire lives, the very happiness they have devoted their lives to attain. It is, in a word," and then he threw it from his mouth, as if spitting upon it, "ignorance, ignorance of how reality actually works."

Since I hardly knew how reality did actually work, and had to admit that the science of understanding this reality must be very backward in my world—since all of us living here would agree that we sought the secret to happiness, and yet the only thing our current state of knowledge had brought us was war and hatred and misery—then I could only guess at what Maitreya was describing. But again, with the touch of his fingertips, I felt I was blessed with a certain understanding: that it was possible that there existed certain laws of reality which, if we could ever comprehend them fully, we could use to free ourselves from all suffering. In a single moment this filled me with both great comfort and great wonder: I was overcome with a thirst to know more of these laws, if I could.

"And do not ever doubt, my love," I was growing accustomed to these expressions by now, and in fact felt a growing attraction to the state of mind which produced them, "do not doubt," he said, "that it is possible to know these things, and that there are beings who know them already, and that they stand ready and willing, all around you, to guide you to this knowledge, and that this knowledge can bring you absolute freedom and happiness; and so imagine, sweet one, spending the rest of your life, free of that skepticism and doubt in the spiritual Path which has sent many intelligent scoffers to their deaths, in absolute and naked defenselessness." I felt that such doubt was no great problem for me, mainly because of my faith in Her and this holy place, and my constant drive to return here to seek my life, but I realized that those few good spiritual habits which any of us might attain are easily lost, and so I resolved to appreciate and defend my surety that there must be a Path, and guides along the Path; whereby I fell into thoughts of Her.

Maitreya respected this diversion, he saw its conclusion far into the future, and remained silent for some time. We bathed in the summer warmth of the roses and tangerine and plum, in the fragrance that the unexpected warmth had coaxed from all the life of the Garden, and I think I must even have slept there, on the grass at the end of winter, under the blanket of pure and indiscriminate love emanating from his mind.

Then his mouth was down close to my ear, and he said, "Tomorrow you will return to your work, and your studies and writing, and in the midst of them, you will recall the words I speak now. You will stop during the bustle of the day, and pause, and imagine finally your mind, freed forever from those most dangerous of all bad thoughts: the intellectual ones, the ones that seek a path, but in a way which is mistaken, and which can send you back into the very darkness from which you have now partially escaped.

"These are ideas like those that say you will not go on after death, or that you have come from no cause in the past; or that there is no connection between the good and bad things we do and the good and bad experiences that afterward come to us; or that harmful ways of acting toward others, or hurting ourselves, or following some indefensible and unexamined beliefs could ever bring us any of our spiritual goals. Imagine at that moment your mind, pure, clean, powerful, seeking, finding, examining, concluding, following—and achieving."

"A fitting dessert," I said sleepily, "to this fine meal you have fed my heart tonight. And I promise," I whispered, "that I *will* make my mind as you say, that I will forever banish from it those negative thoughts and emotions which steal my lifetime and happiness; and that I will follow only the good thoughts, for you have given me the sweet taste of what I could be without them: free, truly free."

I felt his hands on my back, rubbing me briskly up and down, nearly from head to toe, in one innocent outburst of affection. "It is good, dear one, for it has dawned on you tonight what real Freedom is; for it is, as you say, freedom from these poisons of the mind, freedom forever to find and dwell in complete and unending serenity within yourself. But recognizing these poisons for what they are, realizing that these thoughts—which paradoxically we tend to cherish and defend within our being—are actually the source of all our suffering, is not enough.

"On the morrow you will discover, sooner than you think, that you cannot remove these negative emotions simply by deciding to, or even by making some sincere efforts. You will quickly find yourself wanting things, ignorantly; you will see yourself disliking other things, ignorantly; you will be jealous, you will be proud, and you will doubt many things about the Path—even this meeting, myself, and your precious Lady. Oh, you will make progress, and even here tonight you have made progress, and I take joy, for I see you coming closer and closer.

"But in the end there is only one way to remove these enemies, these thoughts, forever from your mind." I knew that this being of light, Maitreya, was about to impart to me the secret of reaching Freedom, and of course this was the aim of my entire existence; but as it happens in such moments, at the most critical junctures of our lives, I was nearly unaware, lulled by the great orb of gold which encompassed both the Garden and my thoughts, and so I barely heard him say, thought I heard him say, "You must, oh please, dearest, you must come to see, for yourself, the holy state of emptiness."

CHAPTER VII

Actions & Their Consequences

The following months were no time to return to the Garden; the enlightening meeting with an Enlightened Being, Maitreya himself, had left me with so much to think about that I could not even formulate my next questions. The entire spring passed while I reviewed the condition of my existence: I spent much time especially reviewing and confirming the fact that the nature of my own mind was that I was incapable of being satisfied with anything I obtained—that within a short time I became restless with whatever new thing I got and wanted something else, whether it was an object or a person in a relationship. I had always assumed that there was something wrong with me, that I was some kind of bad person for feeling this urge to move on, but now I became intrigued by what Maitreya had several times alluded to as the real reason: some kind of forces, some kind of powers beyond my control; "already set in motion," he had said, forces spawning the world I lived in, and myself, and my very thoughts—all sorts of pain and suffering, including this inability to be contented.

When I had asked him about these forces he had spoken only of various thoughts, "poisonous" thoughts, he had called them, which in fact motivated much of my life: jealousy, wanting things, disliking things, pride, and the like. I tried to draw some connection between these thoughts and the sufferings of my realm, but something was missing. I thought, as always, of my mother, the good woman, who had lived for the most part a very good life. She had suffered intensely, as well I knew, from the cancer that eventually ate her heart; but of all the people I had ever met, I felt that she possessed perhaps the fewest of these poisons in her mind: she had rarely displayed anger or jealousy; loved almost everyone she came into contact with, and was loved by them; and made training her children in virtues of mind and conduct a good part of her life's work. I could understand why mental afflictions like envy ruined our peace of mind, but could see no way in which they could cause disease, war, poverty, and death itself.

The hottest days of the desert had passed, although the sun still baked the earth and air, when I next visited the Garden, armed with my new questions. When I arrived I was in no mood for sweet visitations by holy angels, but felt rather like a boxer entering the ring, ready for the jab and parry of true thinking between two people. And I was not disappointed, for as soon as I seated myself on the bench, in through the garden gate marched His Holiness, Gendun Drupe, the first of the Dalai Lamas.

He had taken birth in the rough-and-tumble outback of Tibet, the son of nomad parents, five hundred years before—and his every movement spoke of self-reliance and decisiveness. The first thing one noticed was his powerful chest, fairly bursting out of the top of his robes, and his arms, strong and knotted with muscle, even as he approached his sixtieth year. His eyes were opened wide, almost flaring, with intelligence, and on his forehead were deep creases, tracks that reflected years of deep thinking, and which could have been mistaken for the scars of great sword wounds. In a single motion he crossed to me, waved me off the bench onto the grass before it, and seated himself on it, wrapped in thought, leaving his disheveled robes to fend for themselves.

"What *is it* that runs this world?" he yelled down at me suddenly, leaving me speechless.

He leaned down at me with a fierce, excited, and exciting manner, breathing heavily, almost directly into my face, demanding his answer.

"I don't know, that's what I came to ask, I'm not sure, but I think, perhaps . . ."

"Think! Perhaps! Not sure! Well, I tell you, it's those bad thoughts, that's what! Those bad thoughts, and the actions they make you do! That's what!" and he sat back, triumphantly, as if he had just smashed a worthy opponent in a great debate of philosophy, rather than my simple, flabbergasted self.

I wanted to ask how it all worked, but I was a little afraid to interrupt him, and so held my peace. It seemed to work, for suddenly he burst out again, wagging his finger at me, "We have to figure out the connection: what gets you doing things, and what it is you do, and then how, of all things, the world ends up as terrible as it is!"

I nodded, and waited; he looked down, and deliberated.

"Where do you think it all starts!" he burst out again, just as suddenly.

"Excuse me, what starts . . . how what starts?" I asked timidly. He had this way of throwing your mind off track, or asking the last thing you thought he would ask, and leaving you speechless and flustered as he sat and stared in your face, waiting for the answer that was, of course, quite obvious to himself.

"What makes us do the things we do, and say the things we say?"

I thought for a moment, which luckily inspired me to a fairly speedy reply: "We think. We think to do or say something, and then we do it. Thinking is where it all starts."

The First Dalai Lama's mouth dropped, as if in surprise that I could give the right answer, and then he beamed with a great smile that was ample reward for this and all the other interrogations that some premonition warned me would fill the night before us: "That's . . . right! Right you are!" And he settled back in thought again.

"How many?" he demanded next, glaring at me again and obviously expecting an instant reply.

"Excuse me, how many . . . how many of what?" I nearly whispered, fearing his disapproval.

"Thoughts, of course!" He seemed shocked at my inability to follow his entire train of thought, even though he had neglected to express any part of it in words, just as he neglected his monk's shawl, which by this time—with the constant waving of his arms and heaving to and fro—was strewn all over the bench and the brick below it. "How many thoughts can you have in the time it takes me to snap my fingers?" and he threw his hand at my face, snapping his fingers, as the great debaters have done to rattle their opponents for thousands of years.

I thought, and then had the inspiration to try to time my thought, and came up with about one thought every five fingersnaps. "About five fingersnaps," I replied confidently; "it takes about five fingersnaps to have even a single thought."

He leaned back on the bench and crossed the powerful arms over his barrel chest, which by now had just about entirely escaped his upper robe. His face regarded me dolefully, as if in great pain, with the corners of his mouth pulled down sharply. "Think!" he said. "Think! I don't mean whole thoughts, thoughts that start and end like a sentence, thoughts like decisions or questions. I mean the bits and snatches of thought or impulse that can trigger you to do something, or say something, in a moment of anger or passion! These are the thoughts that start it all! These are the first stirrings of the great forces that create the infinite realms of our universe! Tell me now, and think this time! How many thoughts in the time it takes me to . . ." and again he thrust his fist below my nose, and snapped his powerful fingers with a bang.

Again I was flustered, but this time he wasn't waiting for my answer anyway. "Sixty-five!" he boomed, as if proclaiming a truth that would save the world, as perhaps he truly was. "Your mind completes sixty-five discrete acts of thought in the time it takes me to . . ." He raised his arm, and I closed my eyes, waiting for it to crash down and blast me again, but there was only an eerie pause. I opened my eyes and saw him, his arm still raised, the fingers tightened to snap but never snapped, for his mind had gone ahead, and he had forgotten, as happened so often, to allow his body to keep up.

"And do you realize," he glared at me again, intently, "that every act of thought leaves a discrete imprint, a clear and lasting imprint, upon your mind?"

This seemed reasonable to me, for I knew that certain thoughts, like a strong sensation of anger, had often stayed with me for days.

"Not *that* kind of imprint!" he roared, so experienced in the art of philosophical debate that he could always anticipate the next move my mind would make. "I'm talking about *world* imprints!"

My timidness naturally prevented me from asking him what a *world* imprint was.

"A *world* imprint," he said with a hint of condescension, as if speaking to a small child, which I suppose in a spiritual sense I was for him, "is an imprint in the mind which *creates your world,* which causes you to see every place and every person, and the details of every place and every person, that you ever experience in this life!"

His debater's eyes watched mine, noted the slight sidewise twitch of the eyes as I searched to understand his words, and surmised exactly how much help I needed. "Now imagine," he began, by way of example, "that the keeper of the books in the library where you work during the day has just shouted at you for some mistake you made, right in front of the master of the estate and all the servants. You feel a sharp blast of anger, and then you reply with some angry words of your own.

"Think of that sharp instant of anger as placing an imprint, as planting a seed, on the mind itself. And what do we know about seeds!" he fairly screamed at me again, although by now I was realizing it was simply his manner, and so I relaxed somewhat.

"Well," I said, hoping my answer was the one he wanted,

although it seemed too simple to be, "seeds grow, and then they make plants."

Again he gave me that ultimate reward, that smile of discovery, beamed at me with all the mental power that had forced his body into those lumps of muscle. "Right! You are . . . absolutely right! Good thinking!" and he lapsed again into thought.

"How do seeds act, though?" he said, looking at me askance, as if laying some trap for me.

"Well, I suppose the first thing we can say," I replied without much thought, "is that good seeds make good plants, and bad seeds make bad plants; that is, the seed of some sweet kind of fruit will never produce something like a hot pepper, and the seed from the pepper can never produce a sweet tree of fruits."

His mouth dropped again, as if in amazement, and the eyes lit up. "Right again! Entirely, completely right again!" I felt so good.

"And so if the imprint or seed is planted in the mind by an unpleasant thought, by a harmful thought, then we can say, with complete certainty, that no good result can come of it, that this *world* imprint can never create some part of our world which is pleasant, right?"

This seemed completely logical, and I nodded.

"And the reverse: can we say that if a person thinks a good thought, a kind or compassionate thought, that this could never lead to any negative imprint, but only a good imprint, an imprint which creates some pleasant part of our world?"

I nodded again, for this was equally logical.

"Good!" he exclaimed, as if I had just performed some great and difficult feat. "And now . . . what else can we say about the way seeds act?"

I tried to think of seeds, and remembered the cabin in the mountains, to the north of the desert, where we had sometimes gone as children. A windstorm had pushed a great pine tree down on the cabin roof, and my father had sent me, with axe in hand, to climb the roof and chop off the tree's branches before the rafters gave way under the weight. I remembered my legs shaking, as I am quite uncomfortable with heights. I remembered looking down at my boot, and seeing the tiny sliver of a pine seed fallen from a small cone, stuck there on a raindrop, and thinking to myself that if I had only been there when the seed for this great pine first pushed its sprout from the ground, and plucked the seed up and thrown it on the rocks, then I would not be here now, facing a tree whose weight was perhaps a million times more than that of the seed from which it began. And so I answered the Dalai Lama, "Seeds start small; seeds start tiny; and the things which grow from them can be infinitely larger, millions of times larger, than the seeds themselves."

His arms went up in the air, as if he had just won some footrace against a crowd of mighty opponents, and he boomed with a sound of victory, "Right again! Perfect! Great! And so it is with the seeds of the mind, with the imprints our thoughts make upon our minds: the slightest imprint, with time and nurturing, turns into a massive result, and is responsible for the creation of major events in our world and lives.

"Mental seeds work just like physical seeds, and how could we expect it to be any different? Think of a child, who reads a simple inspiring book, which comes to shape the rest of his entire life. Think of a handful of men, sitting around a table formulating ideas that will shape some great nation for centuries to come. This is the power of the seeds of the mind."

He sat then and glared at me again, and I supposed that he was again awaiting the answer to a question he had once more forgotten to ask out loud; so I thought and ventured a guess, since it seemed that he was pleased whenever I responded at all, but peeved by any hint of silence.

"There is something else," I said, thinking again of the great pine, "about seeds. If they are never planted, then they simply never grow."

The First Dalai Lama began to bounce up and down on the bench, slapping his palms on the terrorized little staves of wood that made up its top. Then he clapped his hands in pleasure, like a small boy. "Just so! If you don't have a bad thought, you don't make an imprint for a bad world. But miss one good thought, and we miss an imprint for a good world. Am I right?" he asked rhetorically, and glared at me again—but I was ready this time.

"I can think of one more thing," I said, encouraged and discovering that by this time I too was up off the grass, balanced on my knees, thrusting my own hands through the air. "Once a seed is planted, if a seed is properly planted, and if the seed is a good seed, and gets all the water and sunlight and nutrients that it needs, then no force in the universe can prevent it from turning into a tree."

He fairly squealed in pleasure: "There you go! So we have four principles of all seeds, those planted in the ground or those planted in the mind: good seeds make good results, and bad make bad; seeds always grow into something immensely greater than themselves; seeds not planted never grow; and seeds planted and nourished properly *must* grow!"

Then he looked away to the side, toward the rosebushes against the north wall of the Garden, and I glanced there too instinctively, thinking that perhaps Another had come. But this was only his way of thinking, and he remained there suspended, half turned, for several minutes. During the silence, a certain series of thoughts repeated themselves within my own mind. I could see how these actions—the thoughts I thought, the words I spoke, or the acts I committed—might leave some kind of imprints upon my mind, but I could not see how such imprints had any influence in creating the very world and people around me. I sensed, though, that he had already anticipated these thoughts, and waited patiently for his presentation. He turned to face me again.

"This is a little difficult," he began, "and you will learn more later which will make it more clear. But imagine for now that your mind is like a clear pane of glass. When you see yourself think some thought, or say or do something, then a tiny stain is put in the glass, like a small dot of color. Imagine, though, that this stain is off to the side of your mind, and you are not aware of it yet. Time goes by, and the stain, the seed within your mind, begins to ripen; that is, it begins to impinge upon your awareness. As it begins to sprout it grows, like all seeds, and soon covers the entire glass of the mind with some patterns of color and shape. Other seeds then go off in the mind in quick succession, covering the glass in a whole kaleidoscope of successive colored patterns, imparting the illusion of motion to the mind. The patterns suggest different objects to the mind: a long form approaching from the door, an oval mouth opening, harsh sounds emitted from the opening, and thus the mind is led to perceive a superior at the library where one works, delivering you a reprimand for some mistake."

I thought for a long moment, and then asked: "I can see how

a single image might be formed this way, say the perception of a single fruit or flower. But the way you describe it, many thousands of mental imprints or seeds must be ripening within even a single minute, given the vast variety of the world we see before us in a single glance, and the smooth flow of time we perceive."

This time there was no answer; he simply gazed into my eyes, and waited for me to understand on my own. And as expected I reflected upon sixty-five discrete imprints pressed into the mind by the fleeting impulses I felt during the single snap of a finger, and then multiplied each one of these imprints or seeds millions of times, in the same way that the weight of the pine seed was multiplied millions of times as it matured into a mighty tree. It was entirely possible then that these imprints could create the many millions of bits of information that were required to create and maintain my impressions of my world for even a minute. But what of the content of these impressions? What accounted for the good experiences in my life, and what for the bad?

My lips separated, I began to speak, but at the same instant he lifted his hand toward his chin, palm out, and I understood that this too I was expected to unravel for myself. Of course! He had already taught me, or I should say, he had already led me to teach myself. If the imprints were good, then the experiences were good; if the imprints were bad, then the experiences were bad. Plum seeds grow sweet plums, lemon seeds grow sour lemons, and it will never be any other way. The pain in my life came from something I had thought, or something I had spoken, or something I had done which was painful, which was harmful to some other being. At that moment whole realms of understanding began to open before the eyes of my mind; dozens of questions, lifetime questions, were answered in a single sweep. Then a doubt occurred to me.

"But what of my mother?" I asked, "a person who was nearly free of bad thoughts, and harmful words and deeds, a person who certainly could never have planted seeds in her mind so powerful, and so terrible, as to maintain for years the perception of cancers tormenting her body, and finally tearing into her heart?"

"But did anyone say," he said with firmness, but gently, "that it was *she* who planted the seeds?"

"Do you mean to say that another person can plant imprints in my mind, and that I am forced to experience the results of another person's actions? It is illogical, it is unjust!" I objected.

"That is not what I mean to say," he said, again with gentle firmness, as if leading me along a great cliff, "for it is totally impossible for us to plant these world imprints in any other mind than our own."

Suddenly it dawned on me—it was a great pain to know it, but a relief to know it, for in this moment I realized another great truth. "How long?" I said simply, knowing he would understand the question.

"These imprints, the world imprints, can in certain cases ripen within the mind, and cause us to see certain details of our world and the people we meet, even before the body dies; that is, before the mind continues on to another realm. But often this is not the case, and so we carry with us in our minds, through death and then beyond, a nearly infinite number of imprints pressed into these minds by the thoughts, words, and deeds of this and our former existences. Your world, your perception of your world, and all the experiences of your life, both outer and inner, were largely set in motion within a past of which you have no conscious memory. And this," he said, gazing down into my face, his intelligent eyes opened wide, glistening with tears, "is why good people suffer."

I nodded, and felt a great sense of release, to find this clear and simple answer, as I had felt it must be, clear and simple, to a question that must have been posed at one time or another by every human mind which ever occupied the very planet on which we sat at that moment. And then another question came to mind: "What is it that makes some imprints or seeds in the mind stronger, and their results more violent, than other, lesser imprints? Why does one imprint cause years of cancerous suffering, and another imprint but a small cut on the finger?"

His somber mood shifted a bit, and the debater began to rise again.

"All life is sacred, and every life is equally important; but would it be more harm to kill a great doctor, who was capable of saving many lives, or to kill a stray dog, for example?"

"It would harm more people if one killed the doctor," I replied.

"And so the imprint would be much stronger," replied the Dalai Lama. "This also applies to those who have been of great assistance to you: your parents, for example, and especially your Heart Teacher. Any help or harm done to people such as these creates an extremely deep imprint."

"This is certainly true of my own parents," I noted, "who were of incalculable benefit to me throughout their lives. But I know of friends whose parents were not so caring, and so I suppose the imprint in their case would be much lighter."

I was met this time with no simple scowl of disapproval, but rather with the entirety of his powerful visage, lit with anger. "It is only with a mind and body such as the one you now possess," he whispered, seeming to control himself only with great effort, "that one can think, clearly, and reason, and learn the spiritual Way, and thus escape from the suffering which has plagued an infinite number of living creatures since time without beginning. And so merely by participating in the creation of such a mind and body, your parents are among the holiest beings in your universe, regardless of their later behavior toward you. Once implanted, imprints are very difficult to change, and so I advise you, if you wish yourself well, to study these matters more carefully, and not make any further blunders of the sort that you have just committed."

He calmed a bit, and then continued: "Other factors make these imprints strong or weak as well. One of them obviously is your motivation. As you have learned, there is a common misbelief in the world that, just because the body stops, the mind stops. People are simply unaware that the mind must go on, and that it most often goes on to some terribly painful place. And so there have been examples, throughout the history of mankind, of people who killed their parents, because they were old and suffering greatly, and perhaps even asked to be killed. When the children do commit such a murder, one of the ultimate murders that a person can ever commit, the imprint is nonetheless somewhat less than it would have been otherwise since their motivation, albeit mistaken, is that they should save their father or mother from suffering. This also applies to cases where we do something by accident, or by impulse, without any clear premeditation.

"As you can see, the planting of these seeds or imprints in the mind is dictated largely by how people perceive the deeds or words or thoughts that they are performing or speaking or thinking, as they are in the very process of doing so. And so another factor is identification: do we realize the true identity of the person that we are helping or hurting? There are, for example, lands in this world where people do not realize that the mind enters the body upon conception, upon the joining of the egg of the mother and the sperm of the father. Again this is because they confuse the growth of the skin and bone and blood of the body with the development of the mind, which is completely different from any physical thing, being invisible, lucid, conscious, weightless, ineffable, immeasurable. And so they do not count it murder when they cause the death of a fetus, for they do not consider this a living thing. Again the imprint, terrible and far-reaching as it will inevitably come to be, is still slightly less strong than otherwise, for these people have failed to identify a living being for what it is. Now you tell me; what else about our intent or motivation might make a particular deed or word or thought more serious than another, leading thereby to a much deeper imprint?"

The hour was advancing, and it seemed that the First Dalai Lama was mellowing slightly, and so I felt less pressure to reply immediately. After some time I said, "I suppose that if an action is committed with very strong emotions—with burning desire or hatred, or with overwhelming compassion and love—then this might make the imprint more strong."

"Right you are!" he roared, and I felt a twinge of chagrin with the lion's reawakening, for it seemed I would have to start thinking a little faster again. "And what about whether you do anything or not?"

I was a little confused. "What do you mean? I thought we were talking about things that people said or did or thought."

"I mean, what if you plan a murder, but never get around to doing it?" he said, with more than a touch of impatience.

"Well then, I suppose there is no imprint," I replied carelessly; but as the chasm opened before me I jumped back. "I mean, I suppose there is only the imprint of the intention and the planning to murder, but not of the actual deed, of stabbing the other person or such." To my relief he allowed my slip to pass, and went on.

"Right. And now, suppose you do strike with the knife. Is the imprint or seed of killing another being planted in your mind?"

"Well, not necessarily," I said. "Suppose the person doesn't die? Suppose he is only wounded, and recovers?"

"Right again!" boomed the Dalai Lama; "and so you see, that for an imprint to be perfect, for a seed, whether it be sublime or evil, to be planted perfectly and deeply, and thus grow into a major event in our future, then the deed or word or thought which plants it must be directed at a significant object; and we must have a clear motivation and premeditation; and we must know the object for what it is; and we must have a steady emotion as we commit the deed; and we must actually undertake the deed; and then complete it as we wished, and be aware of the completion, and take ownership of the deed. A seed planted with all these conditions fulfilled is a deep and mighty seed."

"But can these seeds ever be affected?" I mused. "Are they not like all other changing things; do they not have causes, and are they not affected by factors? Seeds in the everyday world may be planted, and may be very whole and potent seeds, but there are ways in which we can prevent their eventual growth: we can deprive them of sunlight or moisture, we can burn the soil in which they lie, we can dig them up and throw them on bare rock, until they spoil.

"For it seems to me," I said, the victim of a moment's introspection, "that any one of us in just a few hours must have gathered literally thousands of major seeds, and many of them negative, if only in a moment's irritation with a fellow passenger on a coach, or with the slowness of the journey itself. If there is no way to affect the seeds," I worried selfishly, "then surely we must all be doomed to almost endless suffering to come."

"Just so," said the Dalai Lama sincerely, gazing at me in deep thought, too deep to toss me the usual accolades for thinking something straight. "We have many seeds, an almost infinite number of imprints, in the deep recesses of our minds. If we were asked to make a list of the negative thoughts or words or deeds we had accomplished even in the last few hours, we would necessarily omit nearly all of them, since they flash so quickly through our minds and lives—but each and every one of them is recorded precisely and mercilessly in the book of our consciousness. And so any thinking person who had realized the awesome power of these imprints, and the gravity of their consequences, would certainly ask the very question which you have just now."

With a glance he marked the position of the moon, and so for a moment I thought he might leave without answering, but when his face returned toward mine, filled with the traces of that pure white light, I saw a sort of languid, pleasurable look in his eyes which nearly reminded me of someone, but which in any case told me that, even were the Dalai Lama to sit on that bench for the rest of his life, he would do so happily, if it meant that I understood fully the words that he spoke next.

"You must learn the art of cleaning the negative imprints from your mind, and of expanding and accelerating the positive ones to the very point of perfection.

"The latter task I must leave to Another. I will teach you here tonight the first, the art of cleaning negative imprints. If the method I shall describe to you now is followed sincerely, it can remove or reduce to nearly nothing even the most powerful of imprints. The imprint of killing a man, for example, which would normally cause the mind to see one's own self killed, many times, can be reduced to the imprint for feeling a brief, unpleasant headache.

"The cleaning of a negative imprint begins with the act of grounding yourself in goodness. This is done by bringing to mind, consciously, the Enlightened Ones, and your Heart Teacher, and by rededicating yourself to their care, and to the lessons they have taught you, and by remembering the great service you will be capable of rendering to every other living thing, should you yourself master the Path to freedom, and thus become able to impart this Path to others as well.

"The next step in blocking the imprints is to think carefully about the repercussions of the negative thing you have done; for if all we have said in this Garden is true, then any and every harmful thought or word or deed which you ever allow yourself is of greatest harm only to you. This is a kind of intelligent regret, which understands clearly how much pain you are bringing upon yourself by acting or speaking negatively, and not at all like the impotent emotion of guilt which you and your kind so often slip into. Think, think carefully, logically, and clearly, how much harm you do to your own self, whenever you plant a negative seed within your mind.

"The third step is the most powerful, and perhaps the most necessary. It is the touchstone by which you can judge for yourself, in advance, whether the imprints you seek to change have been affected or not. This is your resolution not to continue the kind of thinking or speaking or acting which has caused the imprint to be planted in the first place.

"And at this point I advise you, between us personally," and here the First Dalai Lama smiled at me for the first time as if I were his own son, making all the previous incriminations seem only a very deliberate test of my will and sincerity, "I advise you not to make any sort of resolution that you will *never* commit the deed again; for example, like swearing that you will never again become angry at a superior who was angry to you, because you will not at your current level be able to honor this resolution, and you will only compound the matter, adding to the negative imprint of anger another very serious imprint, one from the act of lying. Set yourself a reasonable time; promise, for example, that you will not reply in anger to him or her for say, the next twenty-four hours.

"Now finally is the fourth step, and this is to choose some action you can undertake as an antidote to the imprint, something to make up for the thing you said, or thought, or did. If for example you had killed some living thing, consciously, in a fight or battle, then you might decide to dedicate some part of the rest of your life to working in a hospital, to serve and protect life.

"But the most powerful antidote of them all," His Holiness said, rising from the bench and gathering at last his robes majestically around his form, "is to learn, to learn to know, the knowledge which can make you and all others totally free of every kind of pain. This begins with the kind of learning and contemplation and meditation you have already found here in the Garden, and reaches its highest form in a deeper understanding of how these imprints work—this concerns the intimate relationship between the imprints and emptiness itself, as you will learn later.

"I have shown you tonight enough for you to realize that imprints planted in your mind by your actions do exist; that they play a major role in creating your very existence; and that they can be, to a great extent, removed from the mind. It is up to you now, to think of all the implications of what we have said here together; think, and think carefully, as if the lives of yourself and others depended upon it."

CHAPTER VIII

Making a World

The meeting with His Holiness, the First Dalai Lama, had for me been perhaps the most significant one of all. As he had foretold, it left me with the raw material for dozens of important realizations about life, realizations which came to me on an almost daily basis as I contemplated our conversation.

I had found in one fell swoop the answers to many of the questions about my existence which I considered most important; for although the concept of mental imprints managing my experiences of my self and my world and the people in that world was difficult at first for me to assimilate, I realized with time that this was merely because of the presuppositions which I had grown up with culturally, and most assuredly not because the concept itself was anything but completely logical, even enlightening.

Above all, the Dalai Lama's words explained perfectly my mother's suffering, and in fact why any good person might suffer, and conversely why people who indulged often in harm to others might, for the time being, appear to prosper. This idea of harm began to reoccur to me: His Holiness had said that painful experiences were the result of negative imprints in the mind, and that these in turn were planted there by actions which were harmful.

But like any thinking person I knew that benefit and harm, good and evil, were no easy distinctions to make; and if the idea of imprints and the world they created were true, then making this distinction between right and wrong correctly became a crucial, even life-saving, issue. And although the answer to the question of the source of my mother's pain was becoming more and more clear in my mind, I had learned nothing of where she might be now, and how I could help her. Lastly I felt as though I were making little progress in understanding the mystery of the Golden One who had first brought me to the Garden, for I sensed that in the end all my questions would be answered if I could grasp the secrets of how She had first appeared, and how taught me wordlessly, and how come to experience that paradisiacal quality that radiated from Her form and languid eyes.

Thus it was that I was drawn yet again to the Garden, in the desert autumn, which is not there known by any great changes in the color of the leaves, or by sudden nakedness and blackness of the branches of trees, but rather only by a gathering bite of the soft winds, by a very gradual increase in the difference between the heat of the daytime and the feeling of the night. Clearly remembering my last meeting at the side of the bench below the carob, I went there directly upon entering the gate, and sat on the grass before the humble wooden seat, as if it were a throne awaiting the arrival of some great King—or even more hopefully, a Queen.

He entered the gate with a stately grace, each fold of his robe in its appointed place, and emanating a graceful propriety simply in the manner by which his left arm was bent, with the carefully folded outer shawl of the monk's habit descending in perfect order to his knee. Even from this I sensed his identity as that of the great teacher of the art of an ethical life: Master Guna Prabha, fourteen centuries removed from his own time, from the golden days of monasticism in the world, but still and forever the perfect monk. He seated himself carefully upon the bench, lifted his legs with deliberation, and crossed them under his vestments, adjusting the robe accordingly, so that it flowed smoothly over his entire form. Then he sat still and regarded me, quiet and powerful.

He was a tall man of strong build, and completely erect despite his age, which I could guess was well into his seventies. Aside from the aura of decorum reflected in his entire manner, the most striking feature was the look of his eyes, opened wide, round, and completely unblinking, as though they belonged to some owl of great wisdom and years. His lips were pursed tightly, suggesting that they were little used to much speech, and his arms completely still, the hands folded on his lap in the gesture of meditation, with the fingers occasionally counting a small rosary there. He sat leaning slightly back, his chin raised a notch, gazing down on me calmly, waiting.

I felt as if I should speak, and so I carefully framed one of the many questions I had carried with me, and then said with a deference that befitted his bearing: "How do we know what is right, and what is wrong?"

He continued to gaze at me steadily, without uttering a word, and then looked down at his hands, cleared his throat, and looked up again, suddenly. "Good deeds make imprints in your mind that make your world pleasant. Bad deeds make imprints in your mind that make your world unpleasant."

"But how can we tell," I continued after a respectful pause, "exactly what kinds of deeds caused the imprints which are making the pleasant things in our present world, and what kinds of deeds caused the imprints which are making the unpleasant things here?"

"Only an Enlightened One," he shot back, quick as a rifle, "can see perfectly what kinds of imprints, and what kinds of deeds which planted these imprints, are responsible for every detail of our lives."

"So then is every single detail of our world, and of our own being and the beings of all those around us, determined by our imprints, dictated by what we said, or thought, or did in the past?"

"Exactly," he replied, and stared down again at his hands and the rosary they held.

"Everything? Every soft breeze of air on the cheek, every line in the grain on a plank of wood, every feature of our faces, the sun, the rising of the sun, the smallest thought which occurs to us?"

"Just so," and again stared at his hands.

"But if we must be an Enlightened One to know perfectly which actions are good, and which are bad, then how can we know which actions to perform that are ultimately good, and which therefore plant the imprints that will make us see ourselves become an Enlightened One?" I persisted.

"Study their words," he said simply, without looking up.

"And if we studied them well," I replied after some thought, "then in theory we could understand exactly those deeds and words and thoughts which would make our future world entirely good, and we could avoid completely those which would cause anything bad in our world."

He looked up from his hands, unblinking, and said sternly, "It is no theory; you can actually do it, and countless Holy Ones of the past have already done so."

"Then teach me, please, what are the actions which will plant the proper imprints, for I am greatly weary of the sufferings of this world; or rather, as I have come to know now, this world which is nothing but suffering."

"Describe to me each suffering of your world, and I will describe to you that action which, according to the Those Who Know All Things, has brought it into existence."

I needed no further prompting. "Death. What action plants the imprint in the mind which causes a person to watch themselves die of a horrible cancer?"

"Killing: the taking of life."

"And so if we avoided ever taking life, human or animal, we would never have to die this way?"

"Just so, except for whatever imprints we may have planted before we began to avoid taking life."

I reflected for a moment upon these old imprints. "And if we purified these imprints from the past, by using the four steps that clean the mind of them?"

"Then you would never have to die that way at all."

This was a rather earth-shaking statement; it contained within itself a kind of holy grail sought after by all mankind since mankind itself began, and left me pensive, with a feeling like that of a person who is experiencing a crucial moment in the history of some great empire, and who is fully aware of how historical the moment is, even as it occurs.

"And poverty; why is it that men can live side by side, in the same country, on the same earth, under the same sky and rain, and some have enough, or even too much, to eat; while others around them are starving?"

"Stealing: taking something which has not been given."

My first impulse, mentally, was that this seemed perfectly logical. But then a certain doubt resurfaced, a nettle which made all this idea of good and bad actions and their imprints seem flawed.

"But I have seen merchants, in business, who stole in a way; that is, they cheated others, for years, and prospered continually."

His chin rose a slight touch more, and he looked down now with the slightest hint of indignation, his eyes unmoving, unblinking.

"And so you have seen sour lemons grow from the seeds of sweet plums?" he asked, almost sarcastically.

"No," I said, "nothing of the kind. It is impossible for the seed of a sour fruit to give forth a fruit which is sweet. Seeds and the fruits they bear are invariably of exactly the same type: sweet give sweet, sour give sour."

"But you just said that a negative action could produce a positive result."

"Well, so it seems," I replied, losing my way a bit.

"Yes," he said, and looked down sadly now at his hands, folded on his lap. "Yes, this is how it seems." He sighed, and continued softly, "And this single fact is the source of the suffering and unhappiness of the entire world, for it seems that by cheating, or by lying, or by deceiving another we can make some profit, get something we want, when in actuality we are cheating ourselves of all happiness, for many years into the future.

"Think carefully now," he said. "Think carefully. Can the fruit tree which grows from a seed appear in the same moment that the seed is planted, or in any time soon thereafter?"

"No, never. It takes time for a tree to grow from a seed; this is the nature of seeds and their results, and in fact the seed is always long gone by the time the tree and its fruits are fully grown."

"And do you have any reason to believe that seeds of the mind should behave any differently?"

"No," I said, and lapsed into thought. Given the urgency which I felt in my own life about these questions, it was but a minute before I grasped what he was trying to tell me.

"According to what you have said," I began, "the only thing which could make a merchant prosper in his business is the act of charity: of giving to fulfill the needs of others."

"Just so," he said, smiling for the first time, pleased with his child student.

"And the only result that could come from cheating others is poverty for oneself," I went on.

He smiled and nodded slightly.

"Then when we cheat someone, and seem to profit by it, we are really only observing two actually unconnected events: the ripening of a positive seed or imprint from giving to others in the past, and simultaneously the planting of a negative imprint for some future poverty, to be experienced only by ourselves."

He nodded again.

Something exploded in my mind—I blurted with excitement, "And this explains, then, why some people seem to prosper when they cheat others, while some people seem to fail when they cheat others, and some seem to fail whether or not they cheat others, and some seem to succeed in either case as well! The world itself does not operate in the way it seems!"

He nodded excitedly himself, and then leaned back again, his chin raised even a touch higher, looking down, as if leading me on toward one more realization.

"If something were really the cause of something else," I said, thinking it through with some difficulty, "then, given the right conditions, it should always and invariably cause that thing. We know, for example, that a corn seed is the cause of a corn plant because, if all the necessary conditions are present, a corn seed will always and invariably produce a corn plant, and no other kind of grain. If cheating in business were the real cause of profit in business, then, all factors being equal, we should always get a profit whenever we cheat someone. But since this is not the case, cheating does not bring us profit. Rather, there must be some other thing which is the true cause of prosperity, and which invariably brings prosperity, all the time, never failing."

"And that is giving to others," he concluded softly, looking at me with the eyes of a very proud father.

In this moment I felt as if the painting of the landscape of my future happiness, and that of those around me, had in a single stroke been nearly completed. It was, I can say without hesitation, one of the few most important moments of my life.

My mind came back then to the sufferings of my world and of those who were passing through it with me. "Relationships," I said. "They seem to be a source of great happiness in this realm, and the source of equal, or greater, pain. We see some couples who live in quiet happiness till death, we see others who get closer, then draw apart, and we see others whose partnership seems doomed from the first moments. What planted the imprint for the unhappy ones to see this happen to their relationship?" I asked.

"A lack of fidelity to one's spouse," he answered without hesitation.

I thought of some examples I had heard of, and hesitated, for I knew of faithful men and women whose spouses had been lost to heartless suitors, but my question answered itself quickly, as soon as I distinguished the current cause for the future happiness, and the current pain of the past infidelity. The logic of Guna Prabha's succinct speech was unassailable. This led me to think of another suffering that had always disturbed me a great deal.

"We see in the world," I began, "some people who speak the truth, and whose words are honored by all. We see others who do not speak the truth, but whose words are honored anyway. Still others speak the truth but are believed by no one, while others speak lies and are equally believed by none."

"Those who are believed spoke truth in the past; those who are not believed lied in the past," he said briefly. "Never let yourself forget the example of the cheater who seems to prosper; do not be fooled by appearances. Use your mind, your sense of reasoning, to see what your eyes by themselves will never be able to see."

I nodded, and continued my inventory of the undesirable parts of life. I remembered that some of my most unpleasant moments had been those spent in the company of people who were constantly bickering with one another, constantly jabbing at each other behind the back, and generally the sort of people whose character was greatly flawed—those kinds of people who, should circumstance throw us in with them for very long, would make our lives a misery and who would—even more serious—begin to affect our own character as well. I asked him the cause of these.

He nodded to acknowledge the question and cast his eyes down once more, picking at the folds in his robes and settling down into a silence. Then he sighed softly and said, "Have you not noticed that people of this realm want others to be their friends and admirers, and should these people befriend or admire someone other than ourselves, how we have an urge to divide or split these two from each other, and so we drop some hint or suggestion that would achieve this disagreeable end? Haven't you realized how often what we say is intended, perhaps more than we are even conscious of, to alienate those around us who have found, for the brief time they are allowed, some trace of friendship and sweetness with one another? This then is your cause, and this is why we so often see ourselves among the low company you have just described."

Again it seemed perfectly logical to me, and I made a mental note to be particularly careful about this kind of talk, since I deeply valued the company of noble people. This reminded me of the irascible keeper of the books in the library where I worked, and so I asked, "And what is the cause of the kind of imprint that makes us hear, from certain people around us, words that always seem unpleasant and confrontational, as if all they thought of was how to pick a fight with us?"

"The cause of this is using harsh words to anyone and, in

fact," Guna Prabha said, with a characteristic shrug as he looked down, "even to an inanimate object: when we speak badly of a neighbor, for example, or curse at a rock on which we have stubbed our toe, or at a delay in the arrival of a coach."

"But what if the person," I began to feel a little defensive, "never thinks that what we say or suggest has any value at all, and makes us feel as though we are worthless?"

"This too has its own cause," he continued immediately, as if anticipating my line of thought, "and that is idle talk, a true bane of mankind, which slowly and surely smothers the entire lifetime of a great many people, while planting the imprints for limitless future misery as well."

I recalled my frequent talks over tea with friends, and reflected upon how much of what we said was sheer wasted speech, so wasted that even a few hours later I could hardly recall what had been spoken. This seemed true as well of all the news we read daily, which would be conveniently forgotten by the next day, so that we could squander more time reading the fresh news.

This took my mind to the sight of the merchants at the inn nearby the library, hunched over the papers full of the latest prices and trends, wrapped in intense conversations and negotiations aimed at amassing wealth, activity so intense and time-consuming it seemed that they often fell ill from nervous diseases, and found themselves either incapacitated, unable to continue their business, or else dead before they could make any significant use of the fruits of their labors.

"And what is it," I therefore continued, "which causes some people's lives to be surrendered entirely to the desire to acquire more and better things; why is it that so many are so little able to find contentment with the sufficiency which they already possess?"

"This is the result of an imprint planted by the emotion of craving: the constant watching after what others have or do or know, and wanting, demanding it, for oneself."

With his words I thought of how I craved the position of the keeper of the books at the library, and craved what he knew of these volumes, not because I sought knowledge that would benefit myself and those around me, but simply because he had these things, and enjoyed them, and I wanted instead that I should have them. Perhaps, I reflected, I should be more help to him, rather than seeking constant minor avenues by which to annoy him.

And so I offered another question: "I know a person," I said, "who has an assistant that is envious of him, and so gives him almost no sincere assistance, and constantly finds ways to make his life inconvenient."

He peered up without raising his head, as if he knew my thoughts, and his partly raised eyelids nearly triggered the image of another face in my mind; something which had happened, I realized, with each of the masters whom I had met here in this holy place. "That person," he said carefully, "is experiencing the ripening of an imprint planted by the emotion of ill will." And with this the normally imperturbable expression of his face distorted a bit: the great owl eyes opened even wider, drawing deep creases across the length of his forehead, and he breathed again a sigh, a deep sigh. "How strange and perverted it is," he said quietly, "that we are so fascinated by the failures of others. Even in a case where we are working closely with someone, perhaps even as their assistant, and where both our fortunes and careers depend on the success of the enterprise in which we are together engaged, we nonetheless harbor this twisted desire to see them fail, and feel so little true sympathy when they do." And he gave me a brief but significant glance, before returning his eyes to their normal home, gazing wordlessly down at his hands, folded upon his lap.

I sat shamefully for a while, looking down at my own hands, but was moved again to speech by a disturbing thought.

"If the trouble given by the assistant is caused by the library keeper's own negative imprints, planted there by the ill will he harbored someone else in the past, then everything is his own fault—it is not the assistant's intention to be troublesome which is giving the library keeper his trouble, it is rather the ripening of the seeds which the keeper planted in his own mind, by himself."

"True, true; although you should also have added the point that the assistant's harmful intentions *will* bring someone the very trouble he hopes to cause—and that someone is the assistant himself."

"So then it's really not even possible for me to be helpful either," I objected, "because if the library keeper does find me helpful it is only because of the helpful things *he* did for others, in the past."

This time Guna Prabha's face shot up at me angrily: "You walk on the very edge of a great precipice; you hold a draft of some great poison directly to your lips. You are about to think a truly evil thought, a thought which has deceived many of the very few who have been fortunate enough to understand what you have, so far, in this Garden.

"Everything you say is true. If we see someone suffering, it is only because he or she has done the deeds, or said the words, or thought the thoughts which would make an imprint in their minds. And this imprint makes them see themselves suffer. So it is true that everyone is completely and personally responsible for even the tiniest pain that ever comes to them.

"It is equally true that, if we attempt to assist them in their misery and we succeed in bringing them some comfort, they feel comfort only because they are now experiencing the ripening in their mind of a different imprint, a good imprint, one that grows into the thing we call comfort.

"But if you mean to imply by this that we therefore have no responsibility to try to comfort others, that it is not our absolute duty and the very reason of our existence to attempt to bring comfort to others, then you have failed in your studies in this place, and you have failed Her and all who have taught you here, and you have failed all those who in the future may benefit from what you learn here, and most of all you have failed yourself, you have failed your humanity. You know in your own heart, even as I speak, that this is true." And I did feel the wrongness of the thought I had nearly allowed myself. Silence ensued after this rare outburst of passion from the reticent master, and I could for some time hear him labor for breath. Then he collected himself and continued.

"Perhaps you should ask me now what it is that causes the great mass of living kind to cling to ideas of their world and their lives which are so obviously wrong and harmful to the happiness of us all. 'What is it,' you should ask, 'that makes people think in ways which so clearly and effectively destroy that very happiness which is the goal of every single thought and deed we ever undertake?'

"The answer," he said, "is allowing oneself ever to have an idea which is contrary to what really brings us what we seek; you have had some taste now of the truth, of what really causes our world, and you can well imagine that the way you used to think, and the way in which most of humanity continues to think, plants the very most harmful imprints of all."

I sat chastened for some time, fearing even that Master Guna Prabha might refuse to speak further, and leave my remaining questions unanswered. He continued to stare downward, counted some unknown prayer over and over upon his beads, and then suddenly looked up again, raising the great round eyes and fixing them in my direction.

"Ask," he said simply.

I gathered my courage and began where my thoughts had left me. "You have spoken so much of these imprints, planted in my mind by my past deeds and thoughts, and you have described, convincingly, how they might affect my personal experiences. But all along you have implied that they create my entire world; by this do you mean as well the outer physical world, the environment in which we live? Are these imprints so powerful that they can dictate those details of our physical world which cause us suffering?"

"Name such a suffering, and we shall see" was all he said.

"I have once traveled to the East," I began, "and visited two very different countries there. They lie on the same parallel, have essentially the same kind of soil and geography, and the same rains and sunlight. In both countries I have seen them plant the very same crops, sometimes even from the same seeds. Yet when these crops are grown in one of the countries, the flour made from the grain seems to have little nutrition; it always seems inferior, dirtier, and the people who eat it remain thin, and emaciated, sometimes even made ill by this food. In the neighboring country the grain produces a flour which is hearty and filling, and makes the people there sleek and healthy. In fact, when I think about it, this is true even of the same medicines in the two countries: in the first land a medicine is likely to be somehow defective, less effective in healing, and at times even poisonous; while in the second country the medicine works nearly all the time, just as it was designed to. What causes this discrepancy in the very countries themselves?"

"Again, it is the act of taking life. The people in the first country killed living things in the past; those of the second did not."

I thought briefly and questioned, "All of this talk about actions and the imprints they leave in our minds has, up to now, given me the feeling that we are personally and solely responsible for the seeds we allow to be planted in our minds. This led me to believe that an imprint can only be planted in a single mind. But now you are talking about the very world itself, the environment in which a great many people live together. You seem to be implying that one huge imprint can be shared by a large group of people."

"It is not that the imprint is shared," he said thoughtfully, respecting the importance of my question. "Rather, it is that a group of people has, as a group in the past, together undertaken some good or harmful action. Each member of the group thereby plants a similar, though slightly different, world imprint, which as it ripens causes each of them to experience a shared reality, such as the inferior crops in a particular region of the world—although just how much this problem with the crops affects each of them individually is slightly different, due to circumstances such as slightly differing motivations when they committed their communal action in the past.

"This, in fact," he said simply, "accounts for the appearance of separate nations, and those invisible and seemingly arbitrary lines between countries called 'borders,' and for the abject poverty on one side of such a border, and the excessive indulgence on the other side of that border."

"So if two countries went to war," I continued, "and if the soldiers of these countries killed one another, then every person in either country who had actively supported this effort would plant in their own minds individual imprints from the act of killing."

"Exactly," he said. "Anyone who supports the effort plants an imprint of the act of killing, as deeply and as firmly as the one who actually pulls the trigger on the front lines."

This led me quickly to another thought, and I said excitedly, "So if one country is threatened by another, by an army which is coming to kill many of its citizens, and if these citizens band together and kill the members of the approaching army instead, then every one of the citizens plants an imprint from the act of killing in their own minds."

"Just so," he said, and looked at me intently, the huge round eyes expanding, until his forehead was nearly gone, waiting for my thoughts to touch gold.

"And the imprints of these acts of killing—wouldn't they, in the future, create the perception in the minds of these citizens of having their lives threatened by something in the future?"

"Say, by an approaching army?" he asked, with a pained smile.

"So can't we say," I hurried, trying to catch up with my own thoughts, "that the very army which threatens a nation has been created by a world imprint planted in the minds of the citizens of that nation when they, as a group in the past, committed the act of killing?"

"Exactly."

A great Sun was dawning in my mind. "And so can't we also say that when a nation responds to the threat of killing by killing, *it is in fact creating exactly the same threat over again, to come at some time in that nation's future?*"

He looked at me triumphantly, his head tilted back almost all the way, as if he were a maestro who had just finished directing some magnificent symphony.

"Then our natural reaction to the unpleasant things in our lives," I concluded, *"is in fact the precise action which would cause us to experience that unpleasant thing again.* The entire world is one big cycle of suffering, perpetuated by our own ignorance, as we do back to others those wrongs which they have done to us!"

He looked at once exultant, and completely saddened, by the truth of my realization. We were silent for some time.

"Then when did it all begin?" I asked. "Who took the first life, so that their life could be threatened, so that they could take life again, only to be threatened again?"

"Why does there have to be a beginning?" he asked, with a question so simple that I often reflected, later on in my life, that this made it the most difficult question of all.

"All things must have beginnings," I objected again; "you yourself would say that all things have causes."

"And indeed they do, which is exactly why our existence, these minds in which we live, have no beginning."

"What?"

"Think about it," he said a bit impatiently; "try to forget what you grew up with; you must have realized by now how much of what you grew up with was simply wrong, simply fables passed from generation to generation without anyone ever checking them. Think carefully now, for yourself. Pretend you are the only person in the world, and you are trying to figure out where your mind came from."

I settled down on the grass, in truth a little angry.

"You have studied the mind already. You know that mind can only come from mind. This invisible, knowing, ineffable, and everywhere-reaching mind can only be produced from something made of the same stuff; that is, from another instance of mind. And you know, for example, that your own mind, at your first moment within your mother's womb, was created from your own mind, which existed the moment before this first moment, in some realm, somewhere. We have already proven this; do you remember?"

"I do."

"So now think of the flow of your mind over a great deal of time: think of it as one moment of mind causing the next moment of mind, flowing into the next moment of mind, in the same way that the immediately preceding moment of this same mind has created the present moment of mind itself."

The wording was a little difficult, but if I thought about it carefully for a minute I could see it: my present mind was the result of my mind the moment before, and my mind in the next moment from now would be flowing from my present mind.

"Now let's check," he said briefly. "Mind is a thing that always has a cause."

"Correct."

"And what is its main cause? What is the thing that turns directly into mind, in the way that a seed turns into a sprout, and clay turns into a ceramic cup?"

"The stuff called 'mind' can only be created by the stuff called 'mind.' "

"And when does the cause of any particular moment of mind occur?"

"In the moment just before it."

"And so," he said, cocking his head with what could have been a hint of conceit in a lesser person, "precisely because the mind has this primary kind of cause, it has no beginning. You cannot point to any particular instance of your mind in the past, even millions of years in the past, and say that *this* particular moment had no principal cause, that it just appeared out of nowhere. Your mind has a primary cause, and that is your mind, and so your mind has no beginning. Get used to it: it is not what you thought in the past, it is something new for you, and it is simply, absolutely true."

Truly it was very difficult to wrap my mind around: the assumptions of my childhood and my entire culture rebelled at the idea. But its implications were clear.

"Then we have forever been responding to violence that came to us because we were violent before, and when we respond with violence we only assure that more violence will come to us again?"

"Exactly. I beg you, do not forget the lesson of the cheater who prospers. Do not believe your eyes in these matters, believe instead your reasoning, which will never fail you. If violence were the true way to resolve conflict, if violence were the cause of peace, then it would always bring peace, for the very definition of a cause is that thing which we know will bring us the expected result if all the other necessary, contributing factors are present. Violence is not the cause of peace because violence does not always bring peace; it's as simple as that."

"And when we respond to violence with violence," I said ruefully, "the only certain thing we are doing is ensuring the perpetuation of that same violence, directed only at ourselves."

He nodded. "Now rest for a moment," he said, for we both needed rest, in our minds and our bodies. And then he sat as an old man sits, bent over, gazing continually at his hands and the beads there, beads that were ever moving, while I shifted and leaned against the carob tree, staring at the stars.

"Not only does the violence plant imprints which beget more violence," he said quietly, almost as an afterthought, turning his head slightly to the tree, "but the very tendency to act in a certain way—to kill or lie or commit adultery—is carried over to later realms in the mind. This explains why even very young children seem to be attracted to different types of kindly or harmful behavior, and makes it doubly difficult to keep ourselves from doing these things as we mature."

I nodded, it made sense, I had always thought that I could see even in the faces of infants certain kinds of likes and dislikes—as if they had carried them from someplace they had lived before—and had noted in my young schoolmates different talents and cruelties that seemed to come to them almost naturally. I leaned back, drained, to feel the reassuring strength of the familiar tree, and looked through its branches again, to catch some light of the stars, and the stars stirred me to one last question.

"But where was my mind," I asked almost in a whisper, "before this planet even existed?"

"You are looking at the answer," he said. "The number of inhabited planets in the universe is infinite. In its own time each planet dies, and in fact the very planet on which we sit now will be burned up as our sun begins to expand well beyond its present reaches, in preparation for its own destruction.

"When the body in which any mind is residing dies, that mind must for a short period of time enter a new body, a kind of spirit form, as a temporary home until the conditions are ready for the mind to perceive itself entering a new body, which of course is caused by a certain combination of imprints in the mind planted by past deeds, words, and thoughts.

"This spirit form is not bound by the laws which govern the matter of normal bodies, and it can move nearly with the speed of thought. Thus it is that a person can enter his next form in another world, another realm, far from the one that you and I see now. And when the last people on any particular planet die before the planet itself dies, their minds move on in the spirit form to one of these other realms.

"I tell you this only for your own information, because you have asked me, and because it relates to our conversation thus far. I cannot show you this spirit form directly now, and so you must investigate further for yourself before you accept it fully, else you would be thinking illogically, and we have had enough of that—am I right?" he said rhetorically and, nodding his head even further, seemed to doze off, while I breathed the night air and tried to collect these many thoughts into my small and tired mind.

When I awoke I was completely lost; I had no idea what time it could be, and it could even have been a different night, for all I knew. I looked over at the bench and saw the old master, Guna Prabha, sitting completely erect, swaying slightly back and forth as if in cadence with some inner spiritual song, staring ahead fixedly, at nothing I could see. I raised myself and, bowing before him, seated myself fresh on the grass at his feet. The swaying stopped, the chin rose a touch, and his great owl eyes regarded me once again, from the great distance of his extraordinary mind.

"We had been talking," I began, "before we strayed from the subject . . ."

"We did not stray," he corrected me.

I nodded; he was absolutely right. "We had been talking about the causes of the world outside of us; the imprints in our minds that determine our very environment."

He nodded.

"I have also been to lands," I said, "where the problem is not only that the food or medicine or other such things have no power to nourish or heal, but further that the crops themselves simply never succeed: they either never come up, or are spoiled by some rust as they stand in the fields, or dry when the rains fail, or rot when the rains pour down too long."

"A result of stealing," he muttered, looking as always down at his hands, "and experienced together by all those in a place who stole."

"And I have been to lands," I continued, "where as one walks down the streets of the cities there stands in the air a fetid stench, always a waft of some foul odor of excrement or filth, a constant string of unpleasant sights and smells and feelings as one simply strolls along any particular way."

"The flowering of an imprint planted in the mind by engaging in various kinds of sexual misconduct," he muttered again, matter-of-factly.

"And I have been to places where no one can trust another, and where no group of people can work well together, and their work always fails, and the very place itself is filled with fear, and things to be afraid of."

"Lying," he said simply.

"And what has made some places flat, and easy to travel and

to build roads upon, while other lands are covered with crags and gullies, difficult to traverse?"

"Engaging in talk which splits up other people," he replied.

"And what has made those odd places of the world where the ground is littered with sharp stones or thorny plants, where there are no streams or lakes, and the entire surface of the earth is parched, dreary, and even threatening?"

"Saying harsh things to others."

"And why are there places where the very trees seem like failed creations, either refusing to bear fruit, or bearing them at the wrong time, too late, too early, the fruit never growing, or rotting quickly; why is it that some towns and cities have many peaceful nooks and crannies, parks and lawns where a person can take their rest, while others are like a jungle of buildings, with no place for respite of body or spirit, and surrounded with dangers?"

"The result of useless talk, of wasted words," he sighed.

"And why in the hands of some people do possessions last long, and retain their quality and usefulness, while when other people manage finally to obtain some object they long hoped for it quickly spoils, or falls apart, or stops working, or works less with every passing day?"

"Craving the things of others; wanting them only for yourself," he said, now picking at his beads, as if perturbed by having to review such a world.

"And why do there come times in the world, and in certain countries and cities of the world, when they are torn by strife, and men kill each other, or terrible diseases spread throughout the populace, or else small creatures like scorpions or poisonous spiders are found under every rock and tree, or larger dangers like the leopard or bear, or the more serious danger of humans themselves wandering amidst the place, waiting to rob or harm those who are simply passing by?"

"Wishing something bad on another person," he said softly, "taking that sickly pleasure in the failures of others."

"And why are there nations or even worlds where harmful ideas begin to spread and take root in the minds of the entire people who live there? What makes a world where the entire population of that world strives after things which can never make them happy? Where people race after possessions and experiences which can only bring them suffering? Where good and healthy and pure ideas, thoughts which can uplift and liberate the human spirit, have passed into darkness, and cannot be turned to by those who cry for this peace?"

"The simple act of living by wrong and harmful ideas," he said, and slumped over, as if exhausted by the effort of viewing these subtle and nearly invisible connections between the deeds, words, and thoughts of mankind, and the consequences of these actions reflected in the world mankind was making.

Thinking of the world as a place where pain and suffering reigned, and ultimately ruined every relationship and person and object, was nearly overwhelming for myself as well, and in my mind I thought of the other realms that the other masters had spoken of. Perhaps there was some hope, and I asked Guna Prabha what world imprints had created these other realms.

He understood my train of thought quickly and, though perhaps unwillingly, punctured it. "Any of the actions that we have mentioned tonight, from taking life to lying, all the way to holding harmful beliefs, has—if committed in a very serious way—

the power to plant a world imprint which causes one to see oneself lost in the darkest and most horrifying torment that exists—pain so intense that you cannot in your realm even imagine it.

"These same actions, if committed in a less serious way, have the power to plant the imprints in your mind that would make you see yourself as a tortured spirit or animal: to look down now where you see arms and fingers, and see instead paws or feathers—and do not think I mislead you, for the mind is eternal and ultimately powerful; if it is capable of maintaining your current uninterrupted perception of an entire world and lifetime, then do not doubt that, twisted slightly by the effects of actions that harm others, it can produce for you the realms I have just mentioned.

"You must understand then," he said wearily, as if pained to tell me more, "that the consequences I spoke of earlier tonight, the effects of what you say or do or think on your personal experiences and your world, were all in the context of your returning as a human being, which is itself caused by almost never committing these actions, and which is therefore, I hesitate to tell you, extremely rare. The opportunity you have now, as a human who is capable of thinking clearly, who can see truly the suffering in which you live, who comprehends its causes and who has at last found the true Path to escape it, is rare beyond all rarity."

Suddenly then Master Guna Prabha seemed to feel a second wind, and he sat up straight, and for the first time released one of his hands from the rosary on his lap, bent it before his erect torso, and pushed it toward me decisively, with the first finger nearly striking my head. "Come now, we have been here nearly all night.

I ask you, as distressing as our talk has been, does it not give you some glimmer of hope?"

I was already thinking along these same lines, as no doubt he knew, which must have been why he had suddenly straightened to ask the question. "I assume," I said with some force of my own, "that if we seek to avoid these harmful deeds and words and thoughts you have spoken of, those actions which plant the world imprints that produce the experience of these realms and lifetimes of disappointment and pain, then we can by the very nature of things avoid the common miseries of these worlds.

"And I suppose," I continued, "that we could go a step further: we could consciously seek to do the opposite of these harmful actions, and thus mold, thus create, consciously, a future world which has none of these sufferings.

"For this I presume that we would have to seek to preserve the lives of all creatures, human or animal; that we would have to strictly respect the property of others; encourage the virtue of honoring one's commitment to one's spouse or partner; speak always and only the truth; strive to bring others closer to one another; use sweet and respectful language to all those around us; talk only of things which are meaningful and beneficial to our lives; take joy in sharing, and in seeing others get what they wish for; hope and work for the success of others in their lives; and finally train ourselves to devote the rare, precious, and numbered moments of thought that we can think in this life to ideas which are of true benefit to ourselves and all those around us. This would plant the imprints for, I suppose, a near paradise, where the exact opposite of all the horrors you have described tonight would greet us at every turn."

"A paradise not only around you," he said happily, animated in a way he had not yet that night displayed, "but within your own mind: the imprints that would cause you to see your own mind as completely pure and peaceful, forever." And then he paused. "But if you really understand now how this can happen, and how it will happen, then I entreat you to listen carefully to what I say next, for this is the true reason that I have come to you in the Garden this night.

"The strength of our negative imprints is mighty, and the few good ones we have were planted there by feeble, impotent, and infrequent good intentions. If you honestly examine your thoughts for several minutes during the course of a single busy day, you will find that the normal pattern is one of a low level of irritation and selfishness with everyone and everything around you.

"To have any hope of strengthening your good imprints to the point where they begin to create your ideal future world, you must seek a way to commit your mind more seriously to what is good—not because someone somewhere is counting your mistakes and wants to punish you later, or anything of the kind, but coldly and truly because you cannot escape this world where everything turns to pain, unless you learn and undertake constantly what is of greatest good for yourself and all those around you. I am talking about taking vows," he said, and I recalled that it was he who had written, over a thousand years before, the great classic on the way to live an ethical life through the taking of vows.

I thought a moment and replied honestly, "Intellectually I understand all we have said tonight, and it is certainly logical to me that I shall have to engage only in good actions, from this night on, if I wish anything good for myself and others. I also have a feeling, from being near you and the other eminent masters who have guided me in this same Garden, that it is also *simply more fun,* and more of a joy, to do what is right, to do what helps others rather than hurting them selfishly.

"But when you speak of vows, the joy somehow disappears, and I think of some kind of restricted and joyless existence, an existence meant for frustrated and unhappy men and women who are incapable of facing up to the challenges of life, and who escape to monasteries and convents where they bottle up their frustration until it becomes a kind of perversion. This is not the kind of life I seek, and I see little way in which it would help me do truly good deeds, which depend so much on being in the world, around other people."

With these words he reached out and touched me for the first time in the entire night, placing his palms with love against the sides of my head, and I could feel for the first time an intense warmth emanating from his body, entering my very mind, reminding me too of Someone else. He looked at me with deep compassion and said, "I admit that you may have met people with vows who act as you have said, although I dare say you might have misjudged them, and should be careful about speaking such words. But this is not what vows are like.

"The art of the taking and keeping of vows has I am afraid largely been lost in your world, and you little understand it. Imagine going to the side of some great and holy being, who is literally overflowing with goodness and the knowledge of sacred things, and kneeling before him or her, and looking in their face, and seeing there the magnificent peace and happiness which is imparted by doing only what is good and pure for oneself and others, and realizing that this intense serenity can be yours as well, and folding your hands at your breast, and saying, 'I swear before you now that I shall be like you, that I will find the happiness you have found.' And then you rise, with your new promise attached to you like some sublime, newfound, mighty wings, and you turn, and step to the window, and fly forth, soaring at will. This is what real vows are like: they are a joy, they are a pleasure, they are freedom from the bondage of selfish and harmful actions toward others, they are enlightened and enlightening, they are light itself."

His face was entranced, and bathed now in the light of the moon, nearly setting, and the stars themselves seemed to be sending down extra golden rays, creating an aura around the outline of his head in the dark of the Garden. I was transfixed as well, and for the first time, without any long explanations, but merely by the overwhelming intensity of the compassion of the being before me, knew that I would take vows.

He glowed even more and smiled down at me. "Begin with the vows of a layperson," he said. "These anyone can take, and they bring joy to any life. You think of the pain that surrounds every object and relationship you have ever known, and to stop this pain, in yourself and others, you swear that you will never again kill a human, or steal something of value, or have sex with the spouse of another, or lie about your spiritual life. You also decide to give up the use of alcohol and other drugs, which I do not need to tell you are an unending source of misery, and an absolute waste of money and time for any person who has the least ability to think clearly about it for even a minute."

I thought for a minute, and asked, "I can understand that it might be good to commit oneself to giving up intoxicants, since they are so widespread and so obviously useless and harmful. But what is the use of taking a vow not to do those other things? Certainly no person with any compunction would want to kill another person, or commit adultery, or lie about the most important subject of all. Why take a vow?"

He straightened and looked me very directly in the eyes. "It is a fair question, and deserves an answer. The imprint which is created when you avoid an action because you have taken a vow to do so is infinitely more powerful than it would be if you had not taken the vow. What I mean to say is, any good deed you do under vows has tremendous repercussions, ultimately powerful effects, powerful enough to purify your mind and world completely. It is much more difficult to do so without the power of vows.

"And making the commitment of the vow helps you keep the vow, and thus avoid any negative, pain-producing imprints. You always remember the holy being who was kind enough to grant you the vows, and when you come close to a bad deed you hesitate, out of love and respect for this being, and this protects you. You remember the reason why you knelt before this being and took the vows, not as some kind of obligation, not as some kind of self-flagellation, but as an act of liberation, of learning to fly, of reaching a kind of happiness that most of the world cannot in the slightest bit even imagine."

And Guna Prabha quietly looked down at his hands, turned

the beads there a few more times, straightened suddenly, leaned back, and raised his chin once more, almost to the sky—then laughed with delight, the beautiful singing laugh of a joyful child, the full and natural laugh of a person who has only done goodness and made themselves, and their life and world, good.

CHAPTER IX

Compassion

The meeting with Master Guna Prabha left me with months of thinking to do. I would walk through the streets of the market in town, or sit at the window of the library, looking out at the fields of cotton and groves of orange, and try to imagine how these could be produced by some seed or imprint within my own mind. It seemed difficult to accept, but during my meditations I reviewed the ideas we had talked about again and again, and could find no fault with them. I knew that Guna Prabha had spoken truly when he said I would have to overcome my natural feelings about what appeared to my eyes, and the prejudices of the culture in which I had been raised, and use instead the sight endowed by careful reasoning.

In time, with continued thinking and observation, I grew accustomed to this new way of seeing things, and it brought me a great deal of comfort that it explained every aspect of my world and my own experiences over the course of a lifetime. Especially when things went wrong—when the keeper of the library shouted at me for some minor error, or when something I had dearly hoped for failed to work out—I reviewed my meeting with Master Guna Prabha, to try to identify what I must have done in my past thinking, speaking, or acting to cause me to see this event.

And I realized that, in every case, the natural reaction which I would have had, such as saying something rude back to the library keeper when he berated me, was exactly the kind of action that would plant an imprint for me to see myself being shouted at again; that is, if I did not restrain myself from my natural negative reaction, I would be perpetuating the very suffering I was trying to avoid.

It became quite clear then that it would make sense for me to take some step that would help me restrain from my natural reactions to wrongs, and so I determined to take the five lifetime vows of a layman. The kindly abbot of the small hermitage where I kept my room granted them to me, with a simple ceremony in his modest quarters.

I truly enjoyed the vows and made it a custom every few hours during the day to review them; it was not that I might have killed a man in every such period of time, but I made it a challenge to find the action I had done which came the closest to endangering the life of another person, or even an animal. Then, in order to achieve a balance within my heart, I also searched the hours to find something I had done in a positive way, something I had done to protect and preserve life, and set aside a few minutes to take joy in what

I had done—for the abbot had advised me that this was a certain way to increase the power of the positive seeds in my mind.

And at the end of every day, before sleeping, I reviewed several of the ten actions that Master Guna Prabha had spoken of, to see what negative thing I had done closest to them, and what thing I had done which was the positive opposite of them. I kept a little diary for this purpose, each day organizing two or three of the ten actions and their opposites like this, on a single page—

1) Taking life

Closest I came to it today: almost hit someone with my horse

Closest I came to the opposite (protecting life): made sure R took her medicine

1. Taking life	*1. Protecting life*
2. Stealing	*2. Respecting others' property*
3. Sexual misconduct	*3. Respecting others' partners*
4. Lying	*4. Telling only the truth*
5. Divisive talk	*5. Bringing people together*
6. Harsh words	*6. Kind and gentle speech*
7. Idle talk	*7. Saying only meaningful things*
8. Craving what belongs to others	*8. Helping others get what they want*
9. Taking pleasure in others' misfortunes	*9. Helping others in their misfortune*
10. Holding on to harmful ideas	*10. Examining my beliefs, and keeping only those that are true and good*

The list of the ten actions and their opposites I kept in the front of my journal, like this—

And so I would write down several instances where I had done or thought or said something that was in any way close to the two or three actions I had chosen for that evening, in both the negative column and the positive column. Within the course of but a few weeks I found something changing in myself and my world.

The first thing I noticed was rather upsetting, for I began to realize that throughout the day, especially as I spoke to others, I was constantly dropping hints, or even making outright statements, that were in a subtle way meant to cast myself in a good light, and to estrange people from others; or else I would say things that, even though I did not use any obviously harsh words, were meant to have the same effect. I began to worry then that I was getting worse, and not better, but the abbot counseled me, and told me that this was a normal impression when someone first started to really watch what they said or did or thought.

The most immediate effect of my efforts was that I simply stopped saying, doing, or thinking things so obviously negative that, even as a novice on this Path, I could not help but notice them. What happened then had little to do with the seeds or imprints that I had learned about; it was much simpler: I simply had more time in my mind for better things, for positive thoughts, and I found myself becoming more creative, better able to concentrate, and in a good mood throughout the day, which was simply very enjoyable. Avoiding bad seeds in my mind was, well, fun, and not the drudgery I'd anticipated when Guna Prabha had first spoken of vows.

In a slower but very steady way, I also noticed my world itself changing, and I remembered that if seeds were planted very consciously and sincerely they could ripen relatively quickly: in an ideal case, one could even alter one's entire reality within this life. The change that started happening to me is difficult to describe, but it was definitely noticeable and real. Foods tasted better, colors were brighter, I felt joy and creativity bubbling within me, and people all around me seemed to begin saying and doing things that inspired my spirit.

I felt instinctively that, if I were able to take this way of life to its final end, then even those things in life which seemed inevitable—such as illness and old age, or death itself—had the potential to change entirely. I also sensed that this greater change would require something more powerful than my present efforts, and so once more I felt compelled to travel to the Garden.

Winter by now had passed, and spring was at its gorgeous height. As I walked through the gate that evening I noticed, perhaps not a little because of my recent practices in the art of a virtuous life, that the small patch of grass had turned to a lush lawn. The fountain seemed to flow with more crystal desert water than ever, and the limbs of the carob tree had spread far beyond the perimeter of the little brick platform around it: they reached out and then down nearly to the endearing little wooden bench where I had learned so much.

I sat on the end of the bench and in the twilight turned my thoughts and eyes to the southern part of the Garden, to a small plum tree under which I remembered standing once with my Golden Lady, drawing a design across Her forehead with my lips, and then suddenly being struck by a sense of concern for people I had never known, and simultaneously feeling a kind of jolt deep within my body. So deeply did I muse on these thoughts that I was unaware that Master Asanga had entered the Garden, and was seated at my side, on the bench.

I turned, and the first thing I saw was his hand, stretched out toward me, holding a small, fragrant *cupsay,* a kind of pastry my mother had often baked for us. "Here," he said, "I heard you like these." He was already munching on one in a friendly way, completely unassuming, and urged me to follow suit. And so we sat there, enjoying the splendid garden and food; each time I finished with one piece, he urged upon me another from a small bag he had pulled from beneath his upper robe.

He looked very different than I would have imagined. He and his half brother Vasu Bandhu, who had already blessed me with his instruction in the Garden, had during the last sixteen centuries been considered two of the greatest thinkers known to us. And yet here before me he seemed simply a very pleasant and friendly companion, with a simple, honest face and a completely gentle manner of moving and speaking, almost to the point of shyness. He wore his robes naturally, not overly concerned about how they looked, but looking therefore as if they were an extension of his very being, so perfectly did their gentle folds match his own evident kindliness.

"Are you all right?" he asked. "Did you have enough? Do you think I might have put too much sugar on them? I tried to powder it, but I haven't quite got it right yet."

I looked at him in amazement as I imagined one of the greatest philosophers of all time fussing over a hot fire to make sure my pastries had been done just right. But this seemed so typical of his nature, and taught me a great lesson even before he began to speak in earnest.

"Time passes," he said gently, looking at me with soft brown eyes, full of concern, "and I find personally that I tend to neglect things of importance."

I grasped immediately that he was alluding to my mother, and my search for my mother, and my journey to find some way that I could help her still, if this were in any way possible. I realized that the pursuit of my own happiness in life had overshadowed my original intentions to help her, and in the presence of such goodness I was forced to flush in shame, and lower my eyes to the top of the bench.

He reached out in a very natural motion and took my hand, as if to apologize for hurting me, but held the fingers with a firmness that told me it was a necessary place to start for the lessons which I needed in my life now.

"Gardens are so nice," he said with warmth. "Have you ever wondered how much thought it takes to plan one properly? One must think carefully, and imagine what would most please every one of the many different people who will ever visit the garden, each seeking some brief moment of serenity in their lives, and finding it in a slightly different way, within a single Garden."

I felt a pang in my chest, and it seemed as though, in these few simple words, he were standing before me, shouting, and accusing me of trying thus far in my spiritual life to build a very strange garden, one only big enough for myself, with no thought of my mother and all the others who needed happiness as well, but who had found no teacher or Path to help them. His extraordinary way of using everyday conversation to draw my attention to the very things I most needed to think about struck me intensely, reminded me deeply of Someone else with a very similar quality.

"Suppose, for example," he continued, as if completely unaware of the way his words were pummeling my heart, "that the person who designed the garden enjoyed plums and roses. I guess that it would take some degree of self-control, and sensitivity, to realize that others might prefer other flowers and fruits. And so the designer of the garden would at some point have to go to other gardens, to observe carefully the people who went there, and try very hard to put himself in their places, and learn to see what *they* enjoy in a garden, almost as well as they do."

Again his words struck a soft point in my heart, and I felt compelled to confess to him, at that very moment, a thought that had troubled me for some time.

"I am not a person who has lived many years," I began, "but even before I had spent much time in this life I quickly understood what a sacred thing it would be if I could really put myself in others' places, if I could truly manage to be as concerned about what they want as much as they were—in short, if I could learn to feel the kind of love or compassion that wants to provide others with what *they* want in life, and wants it every way as much as they themselves do.

"But to be entirely honest," I continued, "I cannot see how it is possible. I am completely aware that I am always infinitely more interested in what I want than in what others want, even if their want is a more serious want, even if their want is a question of their inner or physical survival. I simply cannot imagine any way that I could learn to care for others with the same care with which I care for myself, and this bothers me deeply, for I sense what joy it would bring all of us here in this world if we could learn this one sacred way of living."

"You are completely right," he said with a somber expression, full of concern for my concern. "It is so natural and easy for us to pass through life worrying about those minor needs and wants that we have for ourselves, and ignoring those who may even be dying of hunger and want of shelter, before our very eyes. And as you say, we are aware of this deficiency in our compassion, and I know of few thinking people who do not feel disturbed from time to time by their own inability to care for others with even a sliver of the concern that they automatically show for themselves. We know we want to love, and we know we do not know how."

We sat silently for some time, and I wondered at how close I already felt to him, how he made me feel his equal and even his confidant, within but a few minutes. Then he cleared his throat softly, as if afraid to speak, and said, "I am no great saint . . ."

And in the way he said it, I realized that he was.

"But someone once taught me this meditation that perhaps could help us . . ."

And of course, I knew it would.

"Not that I'm saying that I've been able to do it very well myself . . ."

And I knew that he had perfected it.

"But perhaps you would find it of some use," he concluded. Instinctively I raised my hands to my breast and touched my heart, as if asking him to change it, then and there.

"Prepare yourself for meditation," he said softly, but with the ultimate tone of authority, the authority of love itself. And I prepared myself, within my mind, as I had learned from Master Kamala Shila, here in the Garden.

After a few minutes Asanga said, "Now watch your breath. Watch it pass in and out. Do not try to change it in any way, simply watch it."

This I did, quietly.

"And now think," he continued almost in a whisper, "of some

kind of pain or trouble that you can expect to come to you before this night itself ends."

I could imagine no pain or trouble here in the Garden, especially with Master Asanga by my side, and so I moved my mind later on into the night, thinking of the empty feeling that I always had when I left the gate of the Garden, as I realized once again that I was leaving without having met the Golden One for whom, I had to admit, I still lived.

"And now take that empty feeling," he said quite naturally, "of that future you, of yourself in perhaps an hour from now, and imagine that the feeling has changed to a little pool of pitch-black light, deep in your, his, heart."

I did so, seeing a small blot of pure blackness within myself over there, near the gate, in an hour or so, as he, I, left the gate of the Garden.

"Now wish that you could take that black light away from that future you; make a wish that he would never have to experience that empty feeling, and decide that you will take it away from him."

I made this decision; it was not so hard, considering that I was going to feel better than I would have felt otherwise, if only in an hour from now.

"And now cut that pool of black light away from the heart of the future you, as if with some razor, and decide that you would be willing to take it into yourself now if he would not have to feel it later."

This time I felt a bit of hesitation, a feeling that it might hurt me, but since it was just saving myself the same pain later, I decided I could do so, in the same way that we endure having a cut cleaned out with alcohol, knowing it will help us stop a greater hurt later if we take the smaller hurt now. I decided to accept the black light hurt now.

"Now draw the black light into yourself, suck the empty feeling out of that future you as he walks through the gate over there. Change it to a long thin stream of black light and let it float on the air of your breath as you inhale and your breath returns to your body. If the picture is not clear with one in-breath, then bring the black stream in on several of them."

I did as Master Asanga instructed, and the more I concentrated, the more I felt a slight distaste. But I brought the black light in on my breath, knowing I was helping my future self.

"The breath is entering your chest; the black light is riding on the breath. Now see a tiny flame in the very middle of your heart: this is your own selfishness, and the misunderstanding of your life and your world that creates this selfishness. See, look at the black light, it is approaching that little flame of selfishness; it is about to touch it."

I saw the tip of the thin ray of black light as I breathed it in through my nostrils, and saw it stream down the throat, into my chest, and about to touch the red flame of my selfishness.

"Watch carefully now, concentrate, for it will all be over in a flash. The black light hits the flame; there is a burst of white light; the flame of your selfishness blinks into nothingness; and the black light itself flashes into a puff of thin white smoke that evaporates as well into nothingness—all in a split second. Your own selfishness, and your own future pain, which you decided to take upon yourself, are gone forever, and your heart is clean and pure."

This part was more fun, a happy ending, and I practiced it a few times. Each time I felt a sense of relief, and release, as the little flame was snuffed out and the puff of white smoke faded away.

"Rest for a moment," he said. He pulled a little wooden bowl from a fold at the side of his robes, stepped slowly and gracefully to the spring, and filled it. Then he came and offered it to me, and I drank gratefully, only afterward realizing how natural it seemed that this extraordinary master of philosophy, and of life itself, should be serving a spiritual beginner like me.

He seated himself again, and continued: "Now think of some suffering, some painful situation or thought, that you can anticipate might come to you sometime tomorrow."

This was no great feat, for the thought of the disgruntled look on the library keeper's face as I entered for work perhaps an hour or two late, directly from a late night's ride on the coach, came immediately to mind. I could easily imagine the feeling of resentment that would well up inside of me then, despite my best efforts in the moment, and whatever sincere resolutions I might make in advance, to prevent it.

"Now see the resentment in his heart, in tomorrow-you's heart, as a small pool of black light."

I closed my eyes and imagined it, a black blot inside my chest as I stood framed in the door of the library, facing the keeper's writing desk.

"Now cut it away from your heart." And I did.

"Now be sure to see it for what it is, be sure to think of it as that future pain in your own heart, and decide to take it into yourself.

"Now see it as a thin stream of black light, riding the in-breath, approaching your face.

"Entering your nostrils.

"Seeping down your throat, nearly touching the tiny flame of selfishness and misunderstanding at your heart.

"Touched!

"Flash of white light!

"Selfishness blinks out!

"Resentment gone to a puff of smoke, and the smoke—vanished!" he said urgently.

"Your heart—pure, and clean!"

I felt again the feeling of release, of freedom, and a sort of pride that I was taking care of someone else, even if it was myself. The meditation was having some kind of deeper effect on me, one which I hardly would have anticipated.

"Now try to imagine the three or four worst pains you might have in the whole week ahead. Don't be lazy, define them clearly in your thoughts, and see them as the pool of black light in his, I mean your, heart, a week from now."

This was a little more of an exercise, but I did so. Almost certainly there would be a major insult, or at least a snide remark, from the keeper of the library, one that would stay with me a few days, disturbing my thoughts and sleep. I could probably count on a problem with my horse, he was always losing a shoe or running from me in the morning, when I was already late to the library. No doubt the spring rain would get to the firewood, and my dinner would be late; and, yes, I could, after tonight, expect some sharp feelings of pain, feelings that stayed over the years, remembering my mother, and wondering how I could help her.

"You know the steps," he said. "Now take the pain yourself."

This was something new, trying to keep my mind on three or four different hurts at once, but I could feel that the reward from doing so would be even greater, and I went through the whole meditation slowly, picturing each step clearly. Strangely I felt very relieved that I would have the whole week ahead without at least these few sufferings.

"And now do the whole month," he said. "Define clearly the seven or eight worst things that could come to you in the next thirty days, and go through the exercise yourself. Go slowly, make sure everything is clear."

It took me nearly twenty minutes, but I did as Master Asanga said. On one hand I was becoming more accustomed to my natural hesitation to take on the pain, and I was learning to overcome it; but on the other hand it seemed a larger and more difficult task each time the amount of pain was increased. I caught myself trying not to think of the specific kinds of pain very clearly as the black light approached my face, but I knew instinctively that this was not the point, and so redoubled my courage and pictured them clearly in the black light.

"Enough," he said; "rest again." I leaned back and breathed the sweet spring air, gazed up at the awesome desert stars, and allowed my thoughts to wander the nooks and crannies of the Garden where She had given me other lessons.

Then he leaned over to me warmly, took up my hands in his own, and gazed sincerely into my eyes. "When you have the strength, then increase the pool of black to include the major problems and pains you will face in the coming year. When you are still stronger, visit yourself at your deathbed, and help take away his extraordinary pain. Later on begin to add the suffering and confusion that you will experience just after dying, as you enter that temporary spirit form and begin the journey to your new life. Then take the pains of the entire coming life, and then the lives after that.

"Go carefully, make sure you think of each of the pains clearly, and be very sure to go slowly, do not hurt yourself, take in only what you can do comfortably. It is a good sign if you feel some slight anxiety and hesitation, for it shows that you are really imagining the pains clearly. But at no time, in any meditation, should you push yourself to a point where it hurts, where you become nervous or distraught, for this is very harmful to the heart and to the spiritual body. The key is to meditate regularly, and to build up steadily, little by little, so that the meditation becomes firm and strong, rather than making major but hysterical efforts, for these usually collapse entirely within a short time.

"When your strength is great, your inner strength, then begin to imagine one or two minor sufferings of someone close to you, say your own father or mother. Practice taking these into yourself, and destroying them and your selfishness, along with the misunderstanding that causes this selfishness, in the flash of white light. Then build up to a week with them, and then a month, and so on.

"Move on next to other people that you love, relatives and close friends, as before.

"When you feel yourself even more advanced, then shift over to people to whom you feel neutral: strangers who visit the library, people on the side of the road as you pass.

"When your meditation is powerful enough for a greater leap, then take upon yourself the pains of those whom you actively dislike. This, when you are able to do it honestly, will be a great achievement, an inner achievement, so little recognized by the world at large, which is more impressed if a person can win a battle of strength with a horse than if he or she can win a battle of strength with his or her own bad thoughts and habits, although the latter is infinitely more difficult.

"And then finally, when you are at your peak, send your mind out to every possible habitation of the world: to the houses of humans, to the caves of animals, to the pools where fish live, to the oceans and trees and holes beneath the ground, and imagine every living thing, and practice this sacred act with every outer and inner pain they have. Go beyond your own world to the stars, and to other realms, realms mostly of horror, that your mind knows must exist, although your eyes cannot yet see them. Go, to worlds and planets and realms of hurting things that your mind can barely imagine, and take their black hurt away from them." He sat silently, then raised a corner of his robe, and wiped away his tears, silently.

We sat in the quiet, and I enjoyed the sweet feeling of choosing to notice the pain of others, and wanting to take it from them. I felt at that moment that there was no sweeter emotion in the world—not the pleasure of a lover, nor the thrill of success, nor the fire of power or money.

"Sometimes I think," he began, and I heard coming another one of those lessons that was not a lesson, a teaching disguised as a passing thought, "of how mothers must feel; it is not a feeling that you or I will ever be able to feel in this life, but we can watch and observe mothers, and see their blind and overpowering love for their children, a love that would impel them to commit any act they had to if it meant helping their children.

"This love seems to have two sides to it: there is one kind of love they have that cannot bear to watch their child suffer—you must have seen yourself, a mother with a sick infant in her arms, pushing her way through a crowd of people who wait to see some great physician; a mother racing to protect her child from an oncoming carriage; a mother like a lion rising in fury to anyone who would threaten her child.

"Then there is the side of a mother's love that wants to give, that wants to provide; I suppose we think most naturally of how she wants at the very beginning to give milk, to fill her child with this warm, liquid happiness, and see the contentment on the babe's face afterward. And then throughout her life a mother strives to see to it that her child, even when he or she is already grown, gets everything they wish for: some special piece of clothing, a good schooling, good and helpful friends, and then in their adult years prosperity—a good occupation, a good home, spouse, and their own children.

"The mother wishes all these things on her child in a way that sometimes amazes me as I think of it, because it often seems that—of all the people in the world—it is only your mother who cares for you more than you care for yourself."

And I knew the truth of Master Asanga's words, for this very realization had come to me on the eve of my mother's death, when the winds howled through the trees outside my door at the Academy, and I realized that I had lost the one person who cared more for my happiness even than I did.

"And so," the master said quietly, with a look that was an incongruous mixture of shyness and extreme inner power, "there is a second part to the meditation, which if you don't mind, I can try to describe to you, although I hardly understand it so well myself."

I smiled despite myself, and nodded.

"The entire practice we are doing together tonight is called 'giving and taking,' although when we actually perform it we do the taking part first, and the giving part later. What we take, as you have seen, is the suffering of others, by rehearsing first with our own suffering. Remember the suffering can be anything that hurts a person, all the way from the atrocities that take place in the vast realms of misery—beyond our present sight—on up to the very last moment of doubt, the very last moment before knowledge becomes total, in the mind of a great saint.

"And what we give is all happiness, everything we can, everything we have, as I shall now instruct you. By thinking of how mothers behave you will easily see why the taking comes first, for it would be senseless to offer a child a small sweet, or a toy, if he were at that moment writhing in pain from some disease that was about to take his or her life.

"Now we'll do the giving part," he said, bouncing a bit on the bench, like a child about to play his favorite game. "Prepare yourself for meditation."

And this I did, as before.

"Turn your mind again to your breath, to the flow in, and out, and in again."

I did this almost automatically, as I had been taught, in order to focus myself inward.

"Now picture all your goodness, all your good thoughts and words and deeds, and all the sacred knowledge you have ever learned, and all the imprints lying in your mind that will produce happiness for you in the future. See it all lumped together, as a glowing, pure white light at your heart.

"Next think of someone you know—someone dear to you is easiest to begin with—and think about what they would most like to have, some thing or relationship, or anything else at all."

I thought for a moment and hesitated. My first instinct had

been to send Her something, but upon reflecting I could not imagine what She might want, because in my heart I felt that, when I looked at the way She held her eyes, with the lids half closed in some kind of constant bliss, She seemed somehow complete, and there was nothing more She needed at all. This too, I surmised, was why Master Asanga had not mentioned focusing either side of this meditation on the Enlightened Ones, for there was nothing to take, and nothing they needed. At the same time it occurred to me that I could perhaps at times offer them what little good thoughts or realizations I had reached, as a child proudly shows a parent some little drawing they have made; for I knew that, whatever I chose to send them, they would see and feel it as total bliss itself.

And so I settled on my mother, and imagined that I could provide her with some great lantern, a mystical lantern, which would show her how to make her way away from the realms of terror that her mind might encounter in the time after her death in this world. And as she held the lamp in her hand it would also direct her to this holy Path, like a good horse who knows the way home even after the sun has set and darkness covered the world.

"Now as you watch your breath, focus on one of the outgoing breaths. Do not, by the way, ever try to hold your breath, or control it, during this meditation: it should simply go as it wants to go, without any interference on your part. On one of the outgoing breaths, or several if it feels more comfortable, send forth a slender ray of the white light from your heart, riding on the breath.

"Imagine that the breath flows out into the world, or to the entire galaxy, and seeks out your mother, wherever she may be at this moment. On the tip of the ray of light see your magic lantern; make it full size, for the light rays of thought know no limitation: they can reach to the farthest corners of existence and deliver there any object, from a drop of water to the greatest of oceans.

"Imagine that the ray of light reaches her side.

"Imagine that she looks down, in awe, and sees the white light that has come to her.

"Imagine that she realizes the light has come from you, from her son, and imagine that a great joy, as white as the light, fills her heart.

"Imagine that she reaches into the ray of light and takes up the lantern.

"Imagine that, as we speak, it has already begun to draw her forth, to the greater Light."

While Master Asanga spoke, my heart wrenched with painful memory, and at the same time leapt with sudden hope. "Is it possible?" I asked fervently. "Can she really see it? Does it really go to her?"

He gave me a look of intense compassion, his eyes glistening, and said quietly, "Listen carefully, for I bring you very glad tidings, but not the kind that you may expect. Let me ask you, first of all, a few simple questions. Do you believe in the existence of the Enlightened Ones?"

"Yes," I said. "I may not be able to see them, but more important I understand how they can exist, and I even understand how I might become one. Aside from all this I have an instinct—although I admit that instincts are generally to be viewed with caution, whereas understanding can always be trusted—which has stayed with me throughout my whole life, and throughout my whole being; and this instinct informs me that the Enlightened Ones certainly do exist."

"And do you imagine," he said, "that an Enlightened One is aware of the suffering of those beings who are not yet enlightened?"

"Most certainly so, for they know all things, and our suffering is but one of all things."

"And do you believe that these Enlightened Ones are compassionate? When they see one of us suffering, do they care?"

"Of course they care, they care about our suffering even more than we do."

"And so if there were any way in which they could remove any single atom of our suffering, say by doing this meditation themselves, do not you think that they would have done so a long time ago?"

I sat silent, stunned by the thought.

"And so cannot we say that the fact that we do suffer now is proof that suffering cannot be removed simply by someone wishing it removed, whether that someone is ourselves or any other being in the universe?"

My utter silence confirmed the truth of Master Asanga's words.

"So what is the use," I cried out then, "what is the use of doing this meditation, or anything else? If it cannot really remove anyone's pain, or provide anyone with happiness, then why do we even try?"

He gazed at me somberly. "I ask you," he said quietly. "Why was it that you and I started this meditation in the first place, earlier this evening?"

"I had asked you if there were a way to learn compassion; if there were any way that I could learn to care for others with the same intensity that I care for myself."

"And do you understand why your heart, and the heart of every living being, craves so for this holy water? Do you understand why you thirst so deeply for this ability, this ability to love equally?"

"It is nothing I can put into words, only I sense it to be true, I think we all sense it to be true."

"The real reason," he replied sincerely, "is that with this love we can do all things, and be all things. And there is a part of our mind which realizes this fact, although we are too weak to act on it properly. To put it very simply, this compassion is the one quality that can turn you into a spiritual Warrior. It is the only emotion which can drive you to the greatest height of human endeavor, which is the absolute and unquestioning service of all those around us who need in any way."

"And so actually this meditation cannot help my mother or anyone else," I mused, hardly hearing his words.

Master Asanga grabbed me full on the shoulders, and for the first time he revealed the strength, the overpowering might, of both his body and his intellect. He gave me one powerful shake, and said, "Look in my eyes! Now!"

I looked.

"Think!"

I tried, I was tired, I was beginning to lose the point.

"What would be the logical result of a meditation in which you attempted, if only mentally, to remove the sufferings of every living creature in the universe, and to bring them every wish their hearts desired, from the measly happinesses of the damned existence we live now, all the way up to the highest bliss of total enlightenment?"

I thought for a moment, more clearly under the intensity streaming through his iron arms and hands. "Like all thoughts," I began haltingly, "it would plant a seed or imprint in my mind. But I cannot imagine a more pure intention, nor any thought which could cover a greater object, since we would be wishing for the ultimate happiness not of just ourselves or a few loved ones, but rather for the whole livingkind of the entire universe."

And then it dawned on me. "If I had to choose the one action which could create an entirely perfect world in the future, if I had to choose one thing which could leave an imprint in my mind that would make me see every single detail and person of the world as completely perfect, as pure light, and pure bliss, then it would be the very meditation we are doing tonight."

He nodded, and continued to stare in my face, waiting for more.

"But what good is a perfect world that I have created only for myself if my mother cannot see it? What good is a perfect garden if it is only large enough for a single selfish person?"

"Now listen," he commanded me again. "What does logic tell you? What can your mind find to answer your question? Think! This is why you have come here, this is why the Garden itself exists, this is why you have seen and talked to us, to me.

"When your mother was ill, when the cancer started to eat at her breasts, and then moved to her arms and belly, and finally clawed its way into her heart and released the red blood there over the floor of your entire house, was there anyone who could have come and removed her sickness with a wave of their hand?"

"No, no one, not for her, not for anyone, as long as humanity has lived."

"And what caused her to be ill?"

"According to all that we have said, it was because she herself failed, at some point in the past, to respect life."

"And why did she fail to respect life?"

"Well, because she was like all of us, she was like the entire mass of humanity, who live out their existence, and suffer horribly through that existence, and know no end to this suffering, neither even recognize that the suffering will continue beyond death, nor even often as they suffer realize they are suffering, but continue on like sheep to the slaughter, in fact like sheep that could somehow pick up the knife and slit their own throats—for we suffer because we have caused suffering to others, and we are completely ignorant that this is what brings us our suffering, and because, finally, in seeking to protect what we think are our own interests we respond to evil with new evil, and thus assure evil upon ourselves in the future as well."

"And how is it that you came to know this truth?" he said simply.

"It is the kindness," I said, breaking into tears, "the kindness of yourself, and the kindness of all the teachers who have come to this Garden, to show me that the real source of all pain is the pain we do to others."

"And why did we have to show you? Why did we have to speak, and describe, and reason with you, and make you think, and bring you to a true understanding? Couldn't we have simply taken what we know, and magically put it into your mind, without these hours of heartfelt discussion and contemplation?"

"No, I don't think this is possible."

"Why not?"

"If you love me, you would have done so long ago; I would

have had no reason to come to the Garden, I would know everything already, simply because you wanted me to know."

"And do you think that we understand simply because we understand? Or do you think rather that, once upon a time, at some point in the past, we were exactly like yourself, and knew nothing of the Path, and then had the great blessing to meet spiritual guides?"

"I think you must have been, at some time in the past, just like myself. And then you met the spiritual guides, and you came to understand their teaching, and so finally you reached the ultimate goals of that teaching."

"And so now we have come to the point. I ask you to imagine a world without a single spiritual guide. Think of this Garden as an empty, dark place, with none of the light that you have seen here since that first night, when She granted you the kindness of allowing you to enter this sacred place."

I could not bear the thought. I shook my head violently, and pushed back against his hands on my shoulders.

"And so I ask you; what is the best, and in fact the only, way to help your mother? Do you think you are going to send her a house to stay in, or a bed to sleep in, or some piece of bread or fruit? Do you think this will help her where she is now? Do you think this is what she needs? Do you not know, very well, that during her brief stay in this world she had a house, and that she slept in a bed, and that she filled herself with the mountain of food that a person consumes over the course of a lifetime? And did these things stop the cancer?"

"No, no," I sobbed.

"So what will you send to her, on the white light from your heart?"

"Light, a lantern, a special lantern that guides her to a place without suffering, the lamp of understanding the very things you have taught me."

"And who can be her lamp? Who can teach her truly, the entire Path, from beginning to end? Who sees her whole past, and her whole future, and her whole mind: who knows exactly what knowledge she needs, what steps to lead her upon?"

"Only an Enlightened One," I burst back.

"And what creates an Enlightened One?" he demanded.

"That same thing which creates all things: actions of the mind, actions of the speech, and actions of the body—but to create an Enlightened One these actions must be totally pure, they must plant the seeds in the mind that will make us see ourselves become Enlightened Ones," I said urgently.

"And what meditation is it that plants those seeds most perfectly?" he demanded.

"I can think of none more perfect and complete than the one you have just taught me," I replied, calming within, "because this is the Path to compassion itself, the compassion which loves all others as we love ourselves, better than we love ourselves."

"And so now you tell me," he said, releasing my shoulders, and looking down quietly. "Can you, simply with the power of meditation, take away the sufferings of your mother, and fill her with her every wish, her ultimate wishes—perfect happiness and paradise?"

"If that meditation makes me an Enlightened One, and gives me the ability to go to her and teach her this Path perfectly, then," I said, with a sudden feeling of complete joy, "yes."

"Then send her the white light," said Master Asanga as he rose from the bench, "send the lantern, be the lantern. Send water to those who thirst, become the glass of water. Send a companion for those who are alone, become the companion. Be a lover for those who need a lover, be a child for those who want a child, be a tree for those who wish to sit and rest, be a rose for those who seek beauty, be all things to all people that bring them any happiness at all. Send everything on the white light, out with your breath.

"Our breath moves in harmony with our spiritual body, and changes as a reflection of the health of the spiritual body. The spiritual body in turn is affected by the breath, and as the mind gains in purity both the breath and the spiritual body are made whole. You will find thus that, as the breath carries the light, it will affect you in ways I cannot reveal to you now.

"Devote yourself to this practice of taking and giving. You will find true compassion, but you must practice seriously; whisper to yourself as you move through the day, 'giving and taking'; let it be on your mind, and on your lips, constantly, like the breath itself. You can do this practice anywhere, in the market, as you eat, as you work, as you lie on your bed waiting for sleep. And it will, I tell you, bring you to your paradise, your own garden, where you must go first yourself if you have any hope of finding and helping your precious mother.

"Here now, my son," and he leaned over, stretching forth his hand. "Take the rest of these pastries I made for you."

CHAPTER X

The Warrior

The meeting with Master Asanga was perhaps so far the one that most affected my daily life. To my surprise, I found that I had up to this time taken little interest even in the sufferings that I could fairly well predict I myself would be forced to encounter within a few days, much less those inevitable sufferings that would come with illness, old age, and death itself. In other words, the practice of trying to remove the pain of my future self revealed to me just how much of my life had been spent in denial of the course my life would inevitably take. I and those around me had apparently developed sophisticated inner mechanisms to completely block out any awareness of the very apparent futility of most of our daily activities.

When I felt ready I began to take on minor pains of people who were close to me, and with this I gained another realization, which was that I had simply not taken any real interest in their pains up to that time. Of course I knew it was polite in conversation to inquire after the health of the person we were talking to, and about the well-being of their immediate loved ones. And it was not uncommon to get a response, especially from an older person, in which they described their various ailments and those of their children and grandchildren at some length, but I supposed most of us had just learned to sort of block out hearing these things as well: we took little real interest, I guess, because so long as we and those immediately around us were in a reasonable state of health, the complaints of the older people seemed merely that.

But now I realized that it was inevitable that within a few short years I myself would be sitting describing my ailments to some younger person, who would politely ignore me as I had ignored others. Perhaps, I thought, the whole reason for ignoring others was the unstated belief that there was nothing significant we could do anyway to help shield them from the degeneration and destruction of the body that came automatically as each year in this life passed into the next.

I realized that it was crucial during the meditation on giving and taking that I should clearly define and picture in my mind the specific suffering which I was taking into myself, from either myself or someone else. The simple act of making a list of these pains immediately began to make me more sensitive, and with a healthy pride I saw that, if I kept up the meditation on a regular basis, I could very likely develop that state of compassion which I so admired in those rare people who had already attained it. The thought that I could learn to love others to a degree that even approximated the love I felt for myself was particularly sweet and empowering.

Beyond all this I really did understand that, if I maintained a sincere motivation of wishing to take away the pains of all those around me, and in fact the pains of all the living beings I could even imagine, and in addition to this continued to imagine the sacred act of providing every single living creature with their fondest wishes and ultimate happiness, then I could—according to the comprehensive and convincing explanation I had received in the Garden of the forces which created our world and our selves—actually learn to escape this realm of gradual aging and death, and come to a realm where they simply no longer existed—and then finally, I now had some reason to hope to find my mother and lead her there too.

And so I made the meditation on giving and taking a constant theme of my life, throughout the day, as Master Asanga had advised. No one ever knew what I was up to, I kept the practice to myself, and found an odd pleasure for example in wishing all the things he wished for upon my old nemesis, the keeper of the library. As the months went by I began to catch myself acting out my fantasies, bringing the keeper a cool cup of water from the well outside in the hot afternoon when the sunlight struck our side of the manor, or else finding ways to please him, rather than impede him, in our work together.

Inevitably then he began to respond with similar acts of kindness, and I began to wonder to myself why I hadn't behaved this way with him in the first place; what it was that had blocked me from seeing that the healthiest and holiest manner to spend the day together was to think of each other's needs, and supply those needs as best we could.

During my evening prayers and review of the day I began to realize that, regardless of the ultimate and infinite impact that giving and taking could have on my reality, it was already making a joy of my immediate world.

As always happened, though, I continued to be driven by the thought of my mother, and also by the intense wish to meet the Golden One again, an emotion which strangely never left me, but rather intensified as I began to make real inner progress. I felt instinctively that there must be some way through which I could transform the imagined action of the meditation on giving and taking into some more concrete way of life. And so I traveled again to the Garden, this time in the middle of autumn, which in the desert differed little from early fall, or even summer itself, except for the very gradual cooling of the night air.

I entered the gate there quite late in the evening, as was my usual custom, both due to the long ride in the coach to the town and also because this had been Her and my favorite time, since other visitors to the Garden and to the small stone chapel whose wall made up one side of the Garden would have long since returned home to their families and evening meal. Her innocence was such that She was often simply unaware of how Her clothing covered Her or not, and Her manner so completely free of any desire or guile that few people we ever encountered mistook this liberty for impropriety. Nonetheless She had been intensely private in the lessons She granted me, and when I saw the monk standing below the carob before me I realized that, in all the times She and I had ever entered here, there had never been another person present.

He stood looking at me frankly as I approached, and my eyes studied him as I passed the lovely desert roses on the left and short fragrant plum trees on the right. The first impression was of the very size of his form: he was tall and robust, not thin and not stout, but glowing with some different kind of health—strong and sturdy. As I drew nearer, though, I saw the one thing that defined his entire presence, and this was the look of complete enjoyment in his face, the broad unabashed smile—not the kind of smile that made one wonder why the other person was smiling so broadly so soon, as if unbeknownst to ourselves we had a large stain stretching down the front of our shirt—but rather the kind of smile that immediately made you want to smile along. And I did, and he beamed even more.

How could I ever mistake the face of the glorious Shanti Deva, the master of the art of the daily life of compassionate action, who thirteen centuries before had left us with the ultimate guidebook for a meaningful life? But I had hardly time to dwell on the miracle of actually meeting him before he had bounded forth to meet me, halfway to the tree, and thrown his arm around my shoulders, leading me off toward the pleasant area where the spring from the fountain followed the eastern wall through the blooms of desert plants, enjoying a rare opportunity to dress themselves in rich purples and oranges daily, without the benefit of the infrequent thunderstorm that was usually the only excuse they ever had to appear, and then only for a few hours.

"I understand your frustration," he boomed in a deep, happy bass voice, looking over like an accomplice and spilling the warmth of his smile on me like a glowing lamp. "What's the use of always thinking about some trip you're going to take, but never getting to take the trip?"

I was somewhat accustomed to these impromptu outbursts from the masters of the Garden; I had come to expect that they would seem to know my thoughts, and I had learned as well that, given the extraordinary state of consciousness which they had apparently already attained, it was as good to speak in metaphors as in the realities these metaphors referred to. What I mean is, I understood that he understood that I wanted to learn some concrete ways in which I could act out the baby compassion which was beginning to burn within me; and that I wanted to get down immediately to the pressing business of actually finding and helping my mother, and of solving the mystery of the Lady of the Garden.

All of a sudden he stopped short and clasped my forearm in his, as if we were two soldiers making a pact to stand together to the death. "You have found the heart," he said simply, "now become the Warrior."

His words and the sudden gesture caught me entirely off guard, for I had never in my life thought of the word "warrior" as applying to myself. "Excuse me?" I said, a bit timidly.

"A Warrior," he said with strength, "the ultimate warrior. The Warrior who kills death itself; your own death, and the deaths of others."

From my lessons in the Garden already I knew enough not to think that Master Shanti Deva was joking, or even exaggerating. I stood silent, and prepared myself to hear his words.

"The Warrior," he began, "acts in six different ways; that is, for himself. He acts in the way of the perfections."

"Please teach me these perfections," I replied simply.

"The perfections are deeds that make you perfect; on the day they are truly perfect, you become an Enlightened One, and can truly stop the sufferings of others, and find your own ultimate peace.

"We begin with the act of giving. A Warrior gives all that he has: gives all the things that he has to use, gives all the good he has ever done, gives even his or her own body."

My mind turned to giving. "I do give," I said. "More often than not, I can say honestly, I give what the people around me need, when they need it, from what I own."

"Own?" he said, as though he did not know the word.

"Own, possess. The things that I possess, my possessions."

Master Shanti Deva chuckled gently. "And what do you possess?" he asked.

"My things," I answered, "like my coat, or my books, or my bed or room or horse."

"Coat?" he asked, innocently.

"Yes, my coat, the coat that I wear when it's cold."

"And you possess your coat?" he continued.

"Of course," I replied, a bit impatiently. "If not me, who else?"

"Indeed," he said thoughtfully. "And how is it that you possess your coat?"

"I own it, it's mine to keep or wear whenever I want, and no one else."

"Wear?" he echoed again, quizzically. "You can wear it whenever you want? Keep it and wear it, however you wish?"

"Of course," I repeated.

"And so you can say," he said insistently, "with certainty, that this coat will be with you tomorrow? That you control this coat, completely?"

I paused for a moment to think. Possession means control; I possess my coat because I control it, in the sense that I can keep it or give it away, and no one else can make this decision but me. But could I say that I would surely have the coat tomorrow?

I thought with honesty, and the truth struck me with force: "I cannot say that my coat will be with me tomorrow. The coat can be taken from me by force, or stolen in stealth. It can be torn as I pass an iron gate. It can be ruined by the elements on the road home. It can even," I thought a bit more deeply, "lose its owner. It is the very nature of all coats; they get old, they wear out, they fall apart, and so they are taken from us, or us from them, when we die, and other people pick up the coat and try it on, to see who it might fit, and the coat goes to find a new owner."

"So in fact," he said quietly, "you do not control the coat. Other forces control the coat. The coat comes to you, and the coat leaves you."

I nodded silently.

"And in fact you do not even own your own skin, or your own face or your own name, any more than you own the coat, for they come to you, and are torn from you, regardless of whether you want to keep them or not."

I nodded again.

"And this is why," continued the master, "I spoke of giving away the things you use, for you are only a user, a user for the time being, and no owner, not of anything. Give what you have, and give it now, while still you can give, for everything will be taken from you soon enough."

"What are the things to give?" I asked. "And how do I give them, if I am to be a Warrior?"

"Begin with material things," he replied. "Watch people carefully, put yourself in their place; watch their eyes, see what they seek. Begin with the simple things—a cup of tea, a pair of gloves, even a small piece of bread set out for a bird."

I thought to myself that feeding a small bird didn't seem to require a mighty Warrior; but almost before the thought sounded within my mind he had dropped the armclasp and raised his fist at me, almost threateningly. The first finger was outstretched, and strong tendons rippled up the length of his arm, to where the robe folded over his shoulder. "Only a Warrior," he said with vehemence, "could feed a bird perfectly."

I looked at him blankly.

"Only a Warrior," he repeated, "could look at the bird, and understand truly the nature of the bird, and the nature of giving bread to the bird. Only a Warrior could understand, with perfect understanding, that the act of giving a piece of bread to a bird can be the perfection of giving, giving that brings all livingkind, everywhere, to complete, total perfection. The perfection of the act of giving, for a Warrior, is to give with the total awareness of how the act of giving will create paradise, beyond all death and suffering, for anyone who gives perfectly."

"And how do we give perfectly?" I asked.

"When we give with a perfect awareness that if we give for the purpose of reaching our own perfection, and thus be of perfect service to all others, it plants a seed in us to become this perfection."

"And so if the heart is right, the giving is a perfection?" I asked.

"Exactly," he replied.

Something bothered me about this idea. "So it doesn't really matter what we give, as long as we give with this perfect intent?"

"If you give with perfect intent," he corrected me, "then naturally you also give the best you have; you give whatever is most helpful, and most desired by others, within all the means at your disposal, at any given moment. A warrior is a Warrior not only because he is ready to give his life, but because he does everything to give his life when the time for giving has come."

"And so we must give everything?" I asked.

"Everything, but everything with wisdom. To give more than we are capable of giving, and then regret our giving later, is a great mistake, and so we must give as much as we can, perhaps more than we thought we could give, but never more than our heart can gladly give. Begin small, and build up steadily, and then eventually you will be able to give everything, for it is only by giving everything that we can reach everything, and then truly give all to all who need."

"And is it only things that we give?" I asked again.

"You need hardly ask the question, for you know yourself that the highest gift you can receive is the one which you have been granted here on this holy ground: the gift of understanding what it is that has created ourselves and this world, and of understanding how it may be turned into a world of bliss, rather than a world where every good thing is dragged down into loss and pain."

And then he took me by the arm, as if to lead me on past the dark corner of the Garden, out to where the moonlight cleared the eastern wall and the spring fed the flowers. We had taken no more than a step when he suddenly released my elbow and pushed me a touch to the right; I nearly stumbled but caught myself, and turned in a bit of confusion. His powerful form was stooped low on the ground, his large, oval, intelligent face peering intently into the grass. He reached down with his hand and brought up a lovely crimson ladybug, which turned a little on the tip of his third finger, and spread its wings, and flew.

"There," he said with a laugh, rising up to meet me. "There is the third kind of giving, which is protection. You were about to step on our small friend there."

I stood still and looked down at the grass at my feet, for his words reminded me of a thought that had been rustling for some time in my mind. "But if I had stepped on her . . ." I began.

"Yes?" His body straightened slightly, with the instinct of a debater who had spent years on the battlefield of thinking itself.

"I could not have hurt her, unless she had some imprint in her own mind that would force her to see herself being hurt; an imprint that was planted in her mind, in fact, when she herself hurt someone in the past."

"Just so," he said with evident confidence, like a swordsman who already knew the next three moves his opponent would make.

"And if she did not have such an imprint in her mind, then I could not have hurt her; I would have stepped toward her, and missed her, and she would have flown away unharmed."

"Also true," he said, with a tone of fearlessness.

"And so really," I continued, "you gave her no gift at all, gave her no protection at all. Nothing depended on your action, there was no reason to push me away: everything depended on the imprints she had in her mind already."

"Think more carefully," replied Master Shanti Deva, and he sounded like a man delivering a warning. "Is it any contradiction that you have done all you can to save a being's life, that you have practiced the perfection of giving, without any real power to save that being's life at all?"

"It does seem a contradiction, a complete contradiction," I

shot back immediately. "It seems like an action which is perfectly futile."

"And so do you mean to say," he continued, "that there are no Enlightened Ones at all, no one who has ever reached perfection?"

"I don't see how it follows," I snapped back, for this question did not seem like one that required any careful answer.

"Because according to your thinking," he continued, in a perfect flow, again like a swordsman who had planned his blows minutes in advance, "these beings have never been able to reach the final form of the perfection of giving."

"But of course they have," I replied. "You said it yourself; it is their ability to perform the six acts of giving and the rest perfectly which defines them as enlightened."

"But they have *not* perfected giving," he insisted.

"What are you talking about?"

"They have not, according to you, perfected giving; because there are still people in the world who are poor, and who want. How can they have perfected giving, how can their giving be perfect, if there are still people who desperately need to be given to?"

With this my stream of unexamined words was stilled. I began to think. It began to dawn on me then that the perfection of a virtue consisted not in the accomplishment of the external results of that virtue, but rather in the inner perfection of that virtue, necessarily accompanied by its perfect expression. What I mean to say is, I understood in that moment that if I ever learned to practice charity perfectly, it would not mean that every being's poverty would have to be removed, because the poverty that any particular person experiences is a direct result of their own lack of charity, and will not be changed until they can learn to give. All the same, I could within myself perfect the attitude of giving—I could learn to give all I had, and learn to give it to all who ever lived. But at the same time this did not imply that I could simply sit and think about giving without ever trying to give, because no one could ever have the perfect intention of giving if this intention did not express itself in their every action and thought. And so to Master Shanti Deva I said simply, "I see, I see now."

"Remember it," he said, and moved on with me through the Garden. "Because it is true of all of the perfections; it is the way of the Warrior itself." We walked silently then for some minutes, and I reflected upon the fact that the more I understood, the more I seemed capable of silence, for silence seemed itself to be a reflection of contentment, true contentment, an emotion that radiated warmly from the master at my side. As the quiet passed, I asked him about the next perfection of a Warrior.

"The second way of a Warrior," he mused in his deep voice, "is to live the good life: a perfectly ethical way of life, meaning a way of life that avoids any kind of harm to other living creatures."

"By this," I asked, "do you mean keeping ourselves from the ten hurtful deeds?"

"Yes," he replied. "And as you grow further, you must study and master still deeper and higher codes of life—you must learn daily more of what is good to do, and what is not."

"What other codes of life are there?" I asked.

"You already know the code of ten, and you have, I know, committed yourself to the lifetime code of five. When you are ready you must continue on to the code of leaving the world, a code where you own nothing, and own no one—no house, no family, no possessions except your commitment to the spiritual way of life.

"When you are strong in this code you must take on the entire code of the Warrior, a way of life which is driven by the wish to become an Enlightened One, a way of living in which you move through the world not as an isolated stranger in an unknown land, but rather as the Warrior, as a knight, traveling through your life as though it were a road through some deep forest, and staying constantly on the lookout for anyone who needs you, anyone whom you can help, anyone that you can serve, in any way, providing anything from the smallest assistance to the highest gifts of the spirit.

"And there is yet a higher code than this one, a code which you must in this life come to follow, but this is one which you can learn only from Another, from One to whom you are bound in ways you cannot now imagine. To take upon yourself this code you must find a nearly unbearable love for others, and an equal capacity of devotion."

By now we were well into the moonlight, and on the far side of the spring, even in the night, we could see the small red buds of bloom on tiny round cacti between the stones. We stood serenely together at the edge of the water, looking down, and I felt a deep sense of peace, my mind entering and flowing with the small trickle as though it were some deep sea moving itself to the sea. And then Master Shanti Deva nudged me again, as before, but this time I lost my balance completely, and went sprawling across the water, onto the rocks beyond, grazing my hand across thorns in between the stones. I cursed and turned to stand, and saw him back on the grass, his head turned up to the stars, with deep bass belly laughs sounding into the night. I felt a sharp twinge of hurt and confusion and exasperation with such unexpected events, from so unexpected a source.

I stared at him, unmoving, my eyes demanding some explanation.

"The third way of a Warrior," he boomed, "the third perfection, is just that: the art of learning not to be angry at the very moment when anger begins to blaze. It is perhaps the most difficult of all the spiritual arts; it requires infinitely greater skill than many of the long meditations and similar practices which people are so easily impressed by."

"I think I could have understood the point," I said dryly, "even if you had not almost broken my leg."

"There are two things here I wanted to teach you," said the master, as though he had not even heard my words. "But come first, sit here on this bed of fronds, and dry yourself. Here, give me first those wet shoes."

I sat on the edge of the spring, removed my shoes, and handed them to Shanti Deva, who took them and walked over to a pile of yellowed sheaves beneath a date palm a short distance away; he turned, sat slowly, and waited for me. I stood and stepped toward him, then stopped short in pain, for he had led me across a small patch of briars, in my bare feet.

He regarded me with a mischievous smile and continued to speak, as though he hadn't noticed my predicament at all. "The first lesson is that, as you must certainly have noticed by now in your own life, painful situations can come to you at any moment. Things that upset you, people who make you angry, situations to try your patience are everywhere, surrounding you, and they will strike at the moment you least expect, from the people and things you least expect."

I was making my way across the briars, hardly listening to his words. Too far into the patch to turn back, too far from where he sat to go forward. I stood still and waited for a pause, but none came.

"People whom you don't like are endless. Situations that make you upset are countless. If you got rid of the keeper of the library, there would be another person, inside of a week, believe me, to try your patience. Remember, they are being produced by the imprints in your mind: get rid of one, and another pops up. Escape from a relationship to avoid a bad partner, move to a new neighborhood to avoid some unwanted situation, or run away from work to avoid an unpleasant workmate; but within a short time they will all be replaced."

His prattle was becoming a bit too much for me; I was soaked, and the soles of my feet were afire with pain, and still he did not even look up to notice! "Perhaps," I said, "but I really do believe that my life would be much more pleasant if I could just get away from one or two people, like the keeper of the library, and if I could just make a bit more income, so I could improve my room."

"And what about the horse?" he asked.

"Oh yes, and the horse too; one just a bit more obedient; he is such a pain in the morning, as I try to ready him for the ride when I'm already late," I replied, trying to shift out of the briars to the left, but finding the thorns there even dryer and sharper. I couldn't believe he wasn't helping me.

"And the road home?"

"You're right; I'd forgotten about that. Covered with dust half the time, and rocky going around a third of the way home. Quite exasperating on a day when I'm already exhausted from trying to deal with the keeper of the library." I tried to see if I could clear the ground of thorns below one foot, and then prop up the other on my knee and at least pull out the thorns from the heel and other places where I had put my weight. I had nearly decided that Shanti Deva was not only fully aware of my problem, but was purposely trying to hurt me, and I glanced back toward the spring, with some idea of walking away, if I could get back that far.

"Did you forget that book of notes you've been trying to read?"

Despite myself I set down both feet firmly, with a bit of force. "That book! Who could write such a thing? And on such an important subject! I can't believe someone couldn't have organized it a little more carefully!" And with this thought my patience finally broke. "And couldn't you get up for a moment and help me please?" I demanded.

He was up in a flash, and leapt across the space between us; he really was quite tall, and strong, and the strength at that moment was all focused upon me.

"What are you doing?" he roared.

"I'm trying to get across an entire lawn of thorns, with no help from you!" I hissed.

"No, not that. What are you doing in your mind?" he demanded.

"Trying to think of a way to get across these briars, obviously," I retorted.

"Not that! I mean, do you realize where your thoughts are going?"

I paused, and replied, "We were thinking of some problems of my life, we were thinking about a few major things that . . . if I could change them, it would make me a lot happier."

"But has it not occurred to you that you are listing things

from nearly every detail of your day? Haven't you noticed that the things which bother you, the things that upset or irritate you, form nearly every aspect of your life?"

Again I paused, and again saw he was right. Even if I removed what you might call the first layer, the entire first level of things in my life that irritated me the most, there would still be another layer behind it, and another layer behind that. It was endless and, as I realized in the back of my mind, the problem was not perhaps so much a function of the nature of my life as a reflection of my own mind, a state of mind that would find fault, eventually, with anything ever presented to it.

He stood before me and nodded, as though knowing what I knew then. And then he knelt in the briars and lifted my bare foot to his knee, and began to remove each sharp corner, with perfect attention and care. All this was done in silence, and so naturally that I had no time to reflect how strange it was for one of the greatest persons who had ever lived on this planet to be kneeling in front of me in a thorn patch, loving my wounds as a mother would. His hand brushed over my trousers at the calf, and I noticed the cloth had dried, to a soft warm dry, and my feet felt warm and vibrant, cupped in his hand, as he slipped them into my boots, also completely dried and soft. He stood and said softly, "Walk now to the tree there, and sit with me some. I am sorry if I caused you any pain, but I want you to remember these thorns, and the soaking you had, and the sudden fall.

"The way you are thinking of your world is the way of a fool, and not the way of the Warrior. Stop seeing your journey through your day as some kind of obstacle course, littered with unpleasant people and things and situations that you must try to struggle against. You cannot defeat them all, you cannot confront each irritating person and remove them, any more than you could remove every stone from the road you take from your home to the library.

"This idea in the back of your mind that your life would be much better if you could just eliminate a few of the worst things is an endless trap. If you continue to let this idea stay in your thoughts it will certainly continue to make you unhappy, for it can never come true, and if you think about it for a moment you will be forced to admit this. Your world, at least your world as it stands now, is like this patch of thorns, and no amount of wishing can make it a bed of soft grass.

"Imagine some kind of fool, running here and there in this Garden in his bare feet, dragging behind him huge sheets of leather, throwing them over every patch of thorns, and over every patch of stones or dust, in the entire expanse of this place. And then look down now and watch your own feet, covered in simple leather boots, easily stepping over the briars and bringing you to that pleasant palm over there. You cannot struggle against every unpleasant object and person in the world, any more than you could cover the entire planet in leather; better to wear shoes, better to learn that exquisite art of defeating your own anger, better to learn equanimity."

He drew me then to the seat of dried palm leaves, and we enjoyed the night air briefly. Then a question came into my mind. "But oftentimes," I said, "it feels better, it seems like a release, to express our anger openly, and get it out of us."

He laughed his deep laugh, and looked me full in the face. "Of course there is a benefit to honesty, to informing someone in a sincere and appropriate way when they are hurting us or others, if we have some confidence that this will help the situation.

But the idea that any thought or expression of anger could be something good . . ." He chuckled again. "I suppose you could only believe it if you knew nothing of how imprints are placed in the mind, or had failed miserably to realize how truly destructive anger can be.

"And this brings me to the second lesson I hoped to teach you with the briars. Not only must you learn to wear shoes, but you must learn to see clearly the devastation which anger leaves in its wake. There was a point in the briar patch when you were ready to forsake me, there was a point where you had stopped listening completely, where you were ready to throw away, in a minute, every good and pure thing that has passed between us on this holy night, and all because you felt a little uncomfortable.

"I want you to remember this; I want you to remember how you were ready to walk out of here a few minutes ago; and in the nights to come between you and holy beings who will walk with you further in this Garden, I want you to reflect how, in a moment of rage with Shanti Deva over a few small pricks in your feet and a damp spot on your pants, you nearly gave up what will prove to be the highest reward of a human life. No, you cannot allow anger, even for a moment, for in that moment it can destroy all you have built, and all that you could ever achieve."

He seated himself on the soft fronds, and I threw myself beside him, unconsciously releasing a deep sigh, for I was aware of the truth of what he had said, and how little strength I possessed. He clasped me on the shoulder and smiled, and looked out with me across the Garden; "Be patient, stop anger, stop even that anger which is frustration with what seems to be your own slow progress on this Path. Keep a level head, maintain a flow of equanimity, not only with the outer obstacles and problems, but even with yourself—be kind to yourself, encourage yourself: it is so much better for reaching where you want to be.

"The wise suffer during their spiritual studies, and if you seek only comfort you will never be wise. Be not overly attached to the small pleasures, but seek the highest ones. Learn not only to cope with pain, but to see it as a tool, as a path in itself—it keeps you honest, it keeps you humble, it allows you to feel for others who are less fortunate than yourself. Giving in to frustration or anger can only destroy; learning to live with pain and to use it is a skill that will serve you in good stead all the way to that final day, when you are forever beyond all pain. A true Warrior learns to be unshakable."

We sat some more, and then my little adventure and the long night and, most of all, the strain of learning new things and of examining my heart with honesty all began to drain me—and I fell into a brief sleep. In the sleep I dreamt, and saw myself as a child, and thought of the May Day holiday, something I hadn't recalled in many years. I was sitting at a small wooden desk in the school, and looking out the window in the morning sun at a group of my fellow students, boys and girls dressed in bright spring dress. They were dancing around the maypole, each one holding the end of a colored ribbon that was attached to the top of the pole, singing and skipping in a circle that ran to the left. I was alone in the classroom, and felt attracted to the holiday, but somehow unable to stand and run to play.

Then a kindly monk came in, with dark eyes and a soft smile, and led me to a huge vaulted place, with great high windows pouring in sunlight, and a great smooth wooden floor, shining with polish. And he pushed me gently toward the center of the sunlight and air, and said, "Dance, dance whatever you like, make up your own dance." And I ran into the sun, in the midst of the great empty cathedral filled with radiance, and threw myself into spins, just spins, the dance of a child, thinking nothing, arms thrown out, and head thrown back, laughing. Shanti Deva softly touched my arm; he was standing over me, his great strong body framed in the moonlight, regal in his robes.

"Come now," he said gently.

"I am a little tired," I replied. "Couldn't I sit a bit longer?"

"You could," he replied softly, "you could, but there is no time."

"We have all night."

"You cannot be sure."

"Just a few minutes."

"No need."

"I need."

"You do not."

"Really, just a bit."

"We are going now."

"Where? Why?"

"Your mother."

I sat up sharply. "My mother?"

"Your mother. Come."

"Is she here?"

"I didn't say that."

"Then what do you mean?" I said, rising despite myself.

"She is waiting, she needs you, she wants you to come. Will you rest, or will you come?"

"Come, of course, come." I felt new strength, the tiredness was gone completely, and hope had made me light and joyful.

"I knew you would come," and he stepped strong and quickly

ahead; I had no trouble following. "You are blessed with the strength of goodness; you feel the joy of knowing that you do goodness, you sense the great goodness of rising to serve your mother."

And in truth I felt refreshed in a way I could hardly remember, and in but a few moments we were at the dear wooden bench, at the foot of the carob tree, Her school. Here Shanti Deva wheeled around, the bottom of his robes describing a great arc, and grasped me by the hands.

"This is where it shall be, and soon," he said happily.

I looked into his face with hope, and smiled again despite myself, seeing his own smile shine. "What? What will be?"

"It is on this holy ground," he said, nodding toward the small patch of grass where She and I had often lain, "soon to be made holier, that you will be instructed in the last two of the six perfections, and perfectly so, by someone greater than myself."

I paused momentarily, for despite the long night in the Garden, I knew he had taught me only three of the perfections, and three remained. He had shown me how to give, and how to follow a life of goodness, and how to crush anger—only these three.

"But what of the fourth perfection? Who will teach me the fourth?" I cried, almost afraid that I would lose it.

"The fourth is joy, joy in being good, joy in doing good, the good feeling of being good, and the good feeling that gets you to stand up when you are tired, to go on to do more good: a goodness that once you have tasted you cannot doubt its sweetness. Simply remember your mother, for your mother waits, and every moment that passes without you, every moment she spends in pain and confusion, wherever she is, is a moment in which you must be on your feet, and striving for the highest things of the spirit, so that you can reach her, and bring her these highest gifts.

"It is a path of joy to a city of joy, and a joyful task you have to bring her with you. You have no reason ever to be discouraged, no reason ever to doubt, no reason ever to hesitate, no reason ever to turn back. Behind you is only death, behind and gone forever is a way of life that held only pain in the present, and pain in the future, a life of accumulating things and people that can only be lost again. You are on the right way, you have found the right way—take joy, run forward, find her, dance—dance whatever dance your heart desires." And he laughed again that great full deep laugh, and tears filled both our eyes.

CHAPTER XI

Emptiness

And so I, the quiet bookworm, began leading the life of a Warrior, secretly. It was a truly new experience, a new way of experiencing the world in which I had always lived, for the battlefield of this particular Warrior was the same old library, and my little room at the hermitage, and the alley down which I traveled to go to market for my vegetables in the evening. I really did feel like a different person, for I had a totally different purpose than I had had in the past. Going through life before had seemed like walking down a boulevard lined with shops; I was a shopper, a consumer, looking into the windows to see if there was something I wanted, and then doing whatever was necessary to get what I wanted.

Life as the Warrior was entirely different. I really was a knight in shining armor, and walking on my two little feet was like riding some great powerful horse, and looking around myself at the library or on the road was like viewing some great vista from a seat of royalty: I looked at all my subjects, all my children, around me, and dreamt up ways of serving them, of keeping them happy, and assuring their future and ultimate happiness. I gave them all I could, kind words, kindly looks, a pat on the back, what little money I had, and a few words of encouragement, with as much of the spiritual as I thought they could hear happily; while in the back of my mind I was also offering them great piles of jewels, deep spiritual realizations, all the things in the world that no man claimed his own—the blue of the sky, the sound of the sea, the flowers that grew on every mountain on the planet, and I did so sincerely, although no one ever knew, and I did so with the wish that all I offered they could one day possess, especially enlightenment itself; and above all I found a deep and contented joy growing within myself daily, hour by hour.

As the joy increased my thirst increased, for I knew that my lessons were not complete, and like a horse near water I knew I was near, nearer and nearer, and I felt nearly an obsession to reach the goals I knew now were reachable: I wanted to find perfection, I knew I could reach my mother, I knew she was near now, and instinct told me that I was close enough now to see the Golden One again as well, and that the end of my searching, and the finding of what I sought, and my mother, and the masters of the Garden, and the Golden One would all before long join one with the other. And so I went again to the Garden, thinking that perhaps the night for this had come.

I remember distinctly the date it happened, nothing could

make me forget, it was the twenty-eighth of July, and summer was at its height. I entered the Garden late at night, well after the earth had cooled from the heat of the day, and sat on the foot of the bench beneath the carob, drinking in the sweet smell of the desert breezes, sweet respite from the still and burning feel of the daytime, a feel that struck the face and dried the nose and eyes, like the wind from an oven.

I sat and prepared to enter meditation, going through the preparatory steps slowly, with relish, as though I were putting on a soft old glove, or beginning a conversation with some dear old friend. I was nearly finished when I sensed a motion at the gate of the Garden, and then a small form moving quietly down the row of crimson desert roses along the northern wall. The form stooped at one bush, as though saying a silent prayer, and then moved off again.

I caught sight of the head of a monk, well formed and cropped short, with velvet-like black hair, and then the robes and body followed. I had not seen much more than these brief clues before I found myself involuntarily on my feet, with my palms joined at my breast, bowed in deep respect. I glanced up almost in fear, in awe, for before me was Gautama, the Buddha himself, and although he was nothing like what I might have expected, there was absolutely no denying, and no questioning, who He was.

He was not tall, but only medium in height, and his frame was somewhat slight, and slightly bent, in a kind of modesty that nearly seemed like shyness. His every gesture was simple and graceful, as was his entire appearance, and his robes: clean, graceful, simply hung on his simple form, soft and natural with a lifetime of wear. His age no one could have guessed, I suppose I would say about twenty-seven or twenty-eight, but his face gave no certain clue. It was simple itself, and the first impression, besides the modesty, was one of simple honesty: the eyes were gentle and open, rarely blinking, often down in modesty, and there was a quiet happiness in the way his face was held—in the slight but graceful smile, and the smooth, intelligent face. His skin and the rest were the same as yours or mine, it was not as though he were blazing in light or anything of the like, but there was a different kind of radiance about him, one with no color or shape, a kind of clear warmth that bathed his eyes and face and his gentle hands, all the way down to his humble, bare feet; and this warmth radiated forth and filled the Garden, and bathed my being, and bade me to bow, before One who seemed to neither need nor wish any bow. And I bowed.

"Sit," he spoke quietly, "sit, please sit." And I sat instinctively there, on the grass before the bench, and bowed again sitting, praying that he himself would sit there, on the bench. This he did quite naturally, although with a bit of hesitation, as though he did not consider himself worthy of such a throne. And he sat quietly, looking down at the grass, almost abashed, like a young girl alone before a stranger. We sat quietly.

After some time he reached his hand out toward me, and I saw that he had plucked one of the red roses from the bushes on his way in. He didn't speak, he only held it out toward me, as if asking me to look at it, which I did. No words passed between us, I simply looked at the rose, and have no idea what he himself may have been looking at, for I felt still too much in awe of him to gaze into his face.

He withdrew then the rose suddenly, and put three of his fingers under my chin, and raised my face slowly up to meet his eyes.

And then he said, "Rose," and reached the same fingers of both hands to my eyelids, and closed them, and kept his fingers there. In my mind I pictured a rose, a perfect red rose.

Then his fingers opened my eyes again, and he reached out toward me again, holding the rose, and said, "Do not think 'rose.' " And I tried not to think "rose," I tried not to see the picture I had just seen of the rose, and I looked into his hand again. For just an instant, for just a brief flash, I saw a tiny corner of red, outlined against the dark of the night air, and then my eye jumped and saw something roundish and red, farther down, and finally something green, and thin, and straight. And then in the next moment I was again looking at a rose.

"Again," he said simply.

He let me look at the rose, and then he pulled back his hand, and then he gently closed my eyelids, and then he said again, "Rose." I thought of "rose," there was the outline and color of a rose in my thoughts, and then he gently pushed my eyes open again, and again said, "Do not think 'rose.' " And then he opened his hand before me, and again, for a moment, my eyes danced across some colors and shapes, before an instant later I saw a rose in my mind, and before my eyes.

Then he stooped and touched his finger to the ground, and brought up on the tip of it a tiny black ant. He touched his finger to the side of the rose, and let the ant climb onto the rose; the ant began to race across the petals, leaning out over thin air and then reversing itself, racing across to the opposite side, leaning out into the air, nearly falling off the rose, and then racing farther on again, in obvious panic. Gautama touched the rose to the ground, and the black ant raced off into the blades of the grass.

And then he cupped the rose in his hand, and all I could see was the back of his hand. He held the hand to his face, and opened his deep brown eyes wide, and with his head slightly cocked to the side looked at the rose himself, gazed upon the rose. All I could see was his eyes, but in his eyes I saw some kind of extraordinary contentment, some kind of extraordinary happiness with the rose, and I knew in that moment that he was seeing something that I could never in my present condition ever see: he was experiencing some profound state of bliss triggered by the same thing that I had looked at, and I knew at that moment that it could not be the same thing I had looked at. Gautama closed his hand gently around the rose, and turned those shining eyes to mine.

"For a moment," he said quietly, "you saw the rose before you thought 'rose,' and it was only a few simple shapes and pieces of color. Then your mind thought of these as 'rose.' The poor ant also perceived these same shapes and colors, but thought only 'threat,' and then 'death,' and ran for his life. When I looked at these same colors and pieces of shape, I saw all of eternity, and all the minds of every being in existence, and loved them."

Gautama paused, and closed his eyes, as if waiting for my mind to grasp his words, and then think on them clearly, before he continued. And then he reached out his hand again, and opened it, and asked me, "Who saw this thing right? What is this thing? Is it a rose? Is it the Lord of Death? Is it all humanity, and perfect love?"

In his presence I felt as though my mind were someone else's, as though it belonged to some great and enlightened saint, and I had no hesitation to answer, and no need to answer in words. The thing he had in his hand was each of these things, and all of these things, and none of these things. It was to each of the three beings who looked upon it truly what they saw; it was in sum all the things it appeared to be to all three; and it could never have been three completely different things at once. It was what each saw it to be.

He closed his hand again, and paused again. He leaned and whispered to me, fiercely, "See it now as eternity; see it now as all humanity, and know the perfect love for them that I do." And then he opened his hand again, and in almost a trance of joy I looked eagerly into the palm and saw—a simple red rose.

I closed my eyes in disappointment, and said only, "I cannot."

"I know," he said.

"Why?"

"You know very well; you see only what your mind forces you to see; you see only what the imprints in your mind allow you to see, even though you are looking upon exactly the same thing that I am looking upon, when I see all of eternity, and all of life, and feel all love for it."

I closed my eyes and thought "rose." I opened my eyes and saw "rose." He raised his legs up to the bench and crossed them, under his robes, and went into meditation. I crossed my legs, and I went into meditation. The silence grew. I lost the sounds of the Garden, and then I lost the smells and feel of the Garden, and then I lost the feeling of sitting in the Garden, and then finally I lost the feeling even of thinking, and even of myself. It was perfectly and totally still.

I saw emptiness. And it was only that, and I saw it. There was nothing else.

When it was over things began to come back. I was aware of coming down, and then I was aware of myself again. I was aware then, in that moment, for the first time, that I had seen emptiness.

I knew then that I had seen an Enlightened One, and so I knew then that Enlightened Ones really existed.

I knew then, perfectly, that I would myself become an Enlightened One, in the space of seven lifetimes, and so I knew then that my future lives really existed.

I knew then that the Path was perfectly true.

I knew they would not call me by my name when I became an Enlightened One.

I knew the seven lives would be good, no more real suffering, and surrounded by loving parents, and good and learned teachers, and spiritual friends and teachings, exactly as I needed, without fail.

I knew that what I had seen was true. I could never doubt these things again. I knew I was not mistaken, I knew I was not somehow deluded or crazy. I knew that no one, ever, could say anything that would ever make me doubt what I had seen.

I knew that I knew what every holy book in the world said; I knew that I knew the great ocean of knowledge entirely, as though it were reduced to a teardrop in a child's eye. And I knew the truth of these holy books, and I knew I must give my life to keep them in this world, for others to come after me.

I loved every living thing. A light came out of my chest, a powerful pillar of light, with no color, and it went out, and it touched every living thing, and I knew then that I would always live for each of them, and only for them, and that there was nothing else for me ever to do.

I knew that pictures of the Enlightened Ones were true. I knew we had to care for them. I knew that I must bow down to them, and when it was time to rise, I threw myself on the ground before them.

I knew I had seen a different reality, a true reality, a truly higher and pure reality. I knew there was no thing like this reality in the reality I had known. I knew that the reality I had known was not a pure reality. I knew there was nothing in this reality that could ever be pure. But I knew that, of all the things in this reality, the diamond was one thing that was in some small way close to being pure, purely hard, purely clear, and pure throughout, nearly.

I knew I would die. I knew my mind was not yet pure. I knew my mind was seeing things wrong, and always had, until the moment I saw emptiness. I knew that even now, once I had come down, I was again seeing things wrong, and would continue to do so until I was nearly enlightened. I knew I could read minds. I knew that, if I developed myself carefully, I could perform miracles.

I knew I was now someone different because, of all the people in the world, I had seen emptiness, and I had seen all these other things, and I no longer had to suffer as before. It was over with; I was on my way out, with certainty, with a sweet certainty that I would carry with me forever after.

I looked up to Gautama in gratitude. He gazed down at me, in total silence, and complete joy. He knew everything.

CHAPTER XII

The Angel

After the experience in the Garden with the Buddha, my life changed entirely. Imagine a person who knows everything that will come to them in the future, and has seen the highest things of all; what is left to be done? The effects of what I had seen upon my being continued for many years, constantly becoming clearer, and also causing things to grow within me, understandings and longings, that became deeper and sweeter with each passing year. Early on I felt the need to go to the kindly abbot of the hermitage, and request his permission to take the vows of a full monk. There was no great change in my outer life, but rather it felt as if I had come home, that the life of a monk was my natural condition, and after the ordination ceremony I led a sincere life as a monk, almost unnoticed to myself.

The work in the library took on new meaning: I felt compelled to seek out further knowledge about the things that had happened to me in the Garden, and so I began to read carefully through the great and old spiritual tomes that were kept there. With time, over the years, I came across the holy books that had been left behind by each of the masters of the Garden. The teaching of the razor and the honey I found in the *Guide to the Warrior's Way of Life* by Master Shanti Deva, and the explanation of the truth of pain in the *Great Book on the Steps of the Path* by Tsong Khapa the Great himself. Here too were all the details of the meditation taught by Master Kamala Shila in his own work on the *Steps of Meditation.*

Every additional question I could have on Master Dharma Kirti's proof of the existence of past and future lives I found answered in his *Commentary upon Valid Perception,* in the second chapter. Much of Master Vasu Bandhu's teaching on death I found in the *Anthology on Impermanence,* words of the Buddha himself, and in the death meditation from the *Great Book.* The infinite realms, and realms of terror, to which he had alluded I found described in great detail within one of his own writings, the *Treasure House of Higher Knowledge.* I gained a very thorough understanding of the negative states of mind which Maitreya had taught me to fight from the various works on the perfection of wisdom, and especially his own *Ornament of Realizations,* and the later commentaries written upon it.

The teaching on imprints, and the role that they play in our lives and world, I found covered in depth by the First Dalai Lama himself, in his commentary upon the fourth chapter of Master Vasu Bandhu's *Treasure House.* The very important details of how the imprints are stored in the mind, and how they ripen there, I discovered again in the discussion by Tsong Khapa the Great upon the beliefs of the Mind-Only School, in his *Clarification of the True Thought.* The finer points on an ethical way of life I located in Master Guna Prabha's work called the *Summary of the Discipline,* and in the later explanations of it, especially the one composed by the all-knowing Tsonawa.

The essence of the instruction I received from Master Asanga—that is, the details of the meditation on giving happiness and taking on suffering with the breath—I later found in the *Offering to Teachers of the Sacred* by the first Panchen Lama, and in the exquisite explanations of Lama Dharma Bhadra. More on Master Shanti Deva's teaching on the deeds of a warrior I found of course throughout his *Guide,* and in Master Chandra Kirti's *Guide to the Middle Way.* It was in this book as well, and in the *Diamond-Cutter* of the Buddha himself, that I found some limited description of my last experience in the Garden.

For I did not return to the Garden; and these studies, though short to tell of, engrossed me for some twenty years. It took this long to fully examine, and grasp, and bring within me all that I had seen in those few minutes with the Buddha. I prayed and meditated on a regular basis, I served the abbot of the hermitage, I pored over the sacred texts of the library, and matured in mind and spirit. Over the years, to tell the truth, I thought of my mother less and less—it was a natural part of my life, that my life itself had become the search I'd begun just after she died: I no longer thought so much of simply finding and helping her, but rather had turned my entire days and nights into a path along which I felt I must travel in order ever to see or be with her again. I also had a simple portrait of the Golden One that had been made of Her when She was a child, grasping a small bouquet of flowers and shining as the Sun; I kept the portrait by the side of my bed, and looked upon it often, and knew that She was in the world, and well, and that a time would come when I could be in Her presence once more.

The message came one night late, carried by someone I never knew—a simple folded paper with the words "Come to the Garden," with no signature, although I instantly knew it to be Her hand. As it had been so often in my youth, there was no other clue, no day, and no time, and as in my youth I had to sit quietly, by myself, and think of when it might be that I should come to the Garden. The new moon had passed only a few days before, and I knew that She would not have wanted me to meet Her in that darkness. The full moon was still too far away, and I felt instinctively that She would not have required me to wait so long in this greatest anticipation of my life. And so I determined to be there on the tenth day of the waxing of the moon, which was not so far away, and yet full of the light in which I hoped to see Her perfect face again.

The season was early spring, a time of the awakening, even here in the desert, and it seemed to me fitting, for the twenty years away from the Garden had been, though fruitful in an ultimate way, still somewhat gray and cold, like winter, or the time spent in a cocoon. The feeling and colors of the Garden as I entered reflected the place to where my own life had come: the gate was old and well worn, the bricks and wooden bench were still there, but deepened in color from the years, smoothed gently by the feet and hands of the years. The carob tree looked almost exactly the same, and the fountain as well, still overflowing with the sweet sound of desert water. I sat down on the bench heavily, one part of me tired from the years, while inside my heart raced, and the thoughts and memories and expectation whirled. I rested my head on the palms of my hands and listened, and thought. She did not come, and the Garden became quieter, with the deepening of the night.

I looked down and saw a long seedpod that had dropped from the carob, and leaned and picked it up, and placed it in my lap, and stared at it dreamily as I waited. I had always wanted to bring a gift to the Garden, I had always wanted to bring some small precious thing to offer to the masters here, and yet in all these years there had never seemed anything precious enough; anything I ever thought to offer immediately seemed to me so worthless compared to the priceless things I had been granted here, that I had finally, in all the visits, never brought a single thing for them. But now as I waited it came to me, and I held the pod in my hand, looked at its row of seeds, and swore to myself that I would give them this gift, I would repay their kindness with this: I would take these seeds and plant new trees, in new gardens I would build, for other masters, to guide other disciples, as they had me.

I must have sat for hours, at first impatiently, and then with a peace that became greater. The years of contemplation upon the events of the Garden, and the decades spent in meditation and service, seemed to circle around me like some great primeval wind, speeding round and tightening inward, until they created some strong and solid mass. This was a very clear and unique thought that had been forming for some time in my life, and which gave me hints and intimations of some high truth, and now during the time of waiting for the Golden One suddenly became very luminous, and clear, like a crystal that was making its own light. It began with bringing to mind once again my mother, and the suffering through which she had gone.

I saw clearly now that her suffering had been dictated by past events in her own being: things that she had thought, or said, or done, which had created imprints in her that had forced her to see herself suffer and die as she had. When I thought of the two greatest sufferings in my own life, being separated from her and from the Lady of the Garden, I knew they must have come in the same way. I also knew then that any suffering could be changed, if only the causes for it—the imprints—could be changed, by purifying the mind of the negative imprints of the past, and by filling the mind with new and powerful positive imprints. I could also say, honestly, without any improper feelings of pride, that I had spent the last twenty years of my life in cleaning myself of my negative imprints as well as I could; that I had as well practiced the life of a Warrior, with true and honest effort, within me and on the outside, and thus planted new and sacred imprints of great power. And so I knew, quietly and surely knew, that my life, the reality around me, the reality that the new imprints forced me to see as they blossomed in my own mind, must with certainty begin to change, and transform itself, into a world of light and goodness beyond anything that I could have hoped for when I had started on this path in the Garden as a young man. In short, I knew why the note had come to me, and I knew that I would meet Her, here and now; and that something of ultimate goodness would happen now.

As these thoughts reached their end, an end of great and holy silence, I heard Her footsteps. There was no mistaking them, and I knew they were no one else's. It was not the skip of youth, the only foot-sound that I had ever heard from Her, but rather the measured and confident gait of a strong woman in Her middle age. My heart leapt still more, beating so strongly that I was afraid it might break in that moment, and instinctively I moved off the bench onto the grass, not daring to look up, and heard Her seat Herself.

The heart slowed and I could hear Her breath, and stopped to take pleasure in it, in the fact that She was still alive in my world, and that I could see Her once again. Her scent too poured over me, with a theme of gardenia, a fragrance She had always had, and which I had not smelled since, and which tore at my heart like no sight or sound could have. I felt the spring in the Garden, I reflected on the ending of the winter and the rising of the new Sun, the warmth; I basked in Her presence, smelled and tasted the fragrance, listened to the song of the breath, like a warm breeze coming off the desert in summer. I opened my eyes.

First were Her eyes, gazing down on me steadily, with a tender look, doe eyes, brown, and glistening with the emotions of youth raised to a kind of might by the years and separation. She reached out and took my hand, and I glanced beyond Her eyes to the face.

She was tired, exhausted: time had drained the smooth roundness and replaced it with an angularity, hard cheeks and chin, etched and crossed with lines slashed cruelly by time across the forehead and around the eyes, burned as well into the palms and backs of the hands. There was still the long and painfully beautiful golden hair, but it had thinned, and grayed in spots, and lost the waves and glow of youth. In Her whole demeanor there was a kind of tiredness, in the stoop of the shoulders, and the hard corners of the lips, and the resignation behind the eyes. She had lived a life, some happiness, much hardness, great disappointments—a normal life, the life of my mother—and now She had come near to the end, and had, it seemed, few hopes, few looks ahead, and those few looks not far, and not hopeful. She was an ordinary woman, a mother, a middle-aged housewife, a life of no consequence or wonder.

And yet despite what I saw I was drawn, drawn by the hopes of an entire life, and perhaps driven by the things I had learned and come to know. A thought leapt into my heart, an irresistible thought, a knowledge, one that I could not refuse, but which left me entirely afraid to express it. I knew that She had been the one to bring me to the Garden. I knew that She had been the one to teach me first, and I knew the silent lessons given there were no mistake, and nothing ordinary. I knew that my life had been shaped in the Garden, and I knew that She was no ordinary woman, certainly no ordinary housewife as She appeared before me now. I knew that it was entirely possible that She was an enlightened being, and that She had come to my home in the days of our childhood to win me to Her, so that She and then the masters of the Garden could instruct me. I knew not to believe in the ordinariness before me, and I knew well what I must now do, although a part of me hesitated, feared, doubted. I threw myself down, facedown, on the grass before Her, and then rose to my knees, and grasped Her hands, and threw my face in them, and burst into tears, and cried to Her, "Take me now, please, take me to Your heaven."

I felt the hands withdraw in sudden shock, and Her entire form start back to the end of the bench. I looked up into Her face, to ask, but saw there only horror, and She cried out, "You forget yourself! You are a monk!"

I hesitated for a split second, but the knowledge, the knowledge and prayers of a lifetime, drove me on. I reached out again to take Her hands, and asked again, "Angel, golden angel, please, take me, take me with You, now." And in a flash the hands were torn away again, and I felt a stinging blow across the length of my cheek and face. My head dropped in shame and doubt, and my eyes closed, and I only heard, in a sound of disgust and amazement, "What are you talking about? What's wrong with you? Are you blind? Crazy? Look, look at me. I am no angel, I am a normal woman, and a woman with a husband, and children—a normal woman who has become old, and tired, a woman at the end of her life, a woman who knows nothing and hopes for nothing. Look at me, look."

Again I reached out, and this time She was on Her feet, and the foot came down near my hand, with force and fury. "Stop it! Stop! You are a madman!" She wheeled around, in a flash, but I grasped the hand, and arm, and pulled, and came up upon my knees, and then held on with my other hand, and pulled Her hands into my tears, and begged, a third time, "Please, take me, now, please."

"Look at me!" She demanded.

I could not.

"Look! Now!"

I could not.

"My love, now, look up."

I prayed and looked, and saw Her face, lit in the moon, looking down upon me. It was the true face of an angel, soft, a girl of sixteen years, glowing, gentle, full only of an infinite love, and blurred by the tears. And then it changed, slowly, softly, and Her face then I saw clearly, purely, was the face of each of the masters of the Garden, and I knew it had always been Her there. And Her arms came up outstretched before the moon, like great golden wings, and She came down to me, and covered me in them, protecting me, like some fierce guardian.

And then it was quiet, and only Her old intense warmth upon me, and the sound of my rushing breath and blood in my ears.

And the breathing became calm, in that warmth, serene.

And then all became still, totally still.

And then there was an intense heat, and building, and climbing, until there were two pillars of golden fire, stretching into an empty sky.

And the pillars became one.

And then I am Her, Herself. I look down and see the golden hair, and the slender body, and small soft breasts, all pure light. I turn my eyes around my Garden, slowly, and I see it as She does, and it is perfect, and paradise.

The ocean is a pale soft blue, and it rolls softly in light winds, with soft rounded swells, thousands, and millions, stretching to the horizon, at an infinite distance.

Where the blue meets the sky it turns to a deeper blue, and higher up that blue to a gold; an ever more mighty gold as it rises, until it touches the orb of the Sun, far too bright for the eye to look upon.

And the Sun only stands in the sky, and it only bes there as it is, motionless, shining, being its own nature.

The sea moves. A trillion tiny swirls of water form and reform within ripples within eddies within waves across that infinite expanse. Every swirl for an instant faces the Sun. The light of the Sun sparks there in each, throwing trillions of diamonds across the sea; thoughtless, only by being itself, the Sun is there, in tiny sparks of crystal fire across the sea.

And in that moment I am the Sun. By being, I am everywhere

below me, everywhere on the sea, for those instants of time that my fire appears in each tiny swirl. And each brief flash of the light of the Sun on the sea is an entire world, teeming with life, crossed and recrossed by men and creatures as they are born and live and die, in their endless search for happiness.

I seek in each of these infinite worlds my mother.

I look upon the face of each creature, I seek her face.

I can find no one who is not her. And so I shine upon them all, and bring each one my warmth, and feed there, in each new Garden, the seed of the carob tree.

Come touch the Sun.

BY THE SAME AUTHOR

The Diamond Cutter:
The Buddha on Managing Your Business and Your Life

The Tibetan Book of Yoga

How Yoga Works:
Healing Yourself and Others with the Yoga Sutra

The Karma of Love:
100 Answers for Your Relationship, from the Ancient Wisdom

Katrin:
Girls Do Do that

The 36 Books of the Foundation Series
Asian Classics Institute

The 10 Meditation Modules
Asian Classics Institute

Sunlight on Suchness:
The Meaning of the Heart Sutra

Sunlight on the Path to Freedom:
A Commentary to The Diamond Cutter Sutra

Emptiness Meditations:
Learning How to See that Nothing Is Itself

All the Kinds of Karma:
The correlations between our actions & their consequences
according to the Buddha

The Golden Key:
Difficult Questions in the Mind Only School of Buddhism.
Part One.

A Door to Emptiness:
The Crucial Teaching for Touching the Diamond World

The Two Sutras of Medicine Buddha

Great Ideas of the East:
A Survey of 101 Enlightening Belief Systems from Ancient Asia

Stopping the Circle of Sadness:
The Buddhist Teaching of the Wheel of Life

Nothing is the Way It Seams:
The Sixty Verses of Nagarjuna

Deathless Nectar for Helping Others:
The Crown of Knifes

Poems of the Diamond Way

Door to the Diamond Way:
A Guide to Higher Happiness

The Principal Teachings of Buddhism

China Love You:
The Death of Global Competition

King of the Dharma:
The Illustrated Life of Je Tsongkapa